Locked out!

I was so excited coming home. I let myself in with my key. That part was a breeze. I sat down on a chair at the kitchen table, but I was too excited about being a latchkey kid to just hang out. I felt like I should be doing something to show I was this new, super-mature, super-responsible person.

The wastebasket next to the sink was overflowing, and the cats' litter in the basement needed changing. I got both the garbage and the litter into one giant trash bag and put on my jacket and went out back to put the bag in the trash can.

I was trying to keep the cats in, and so pulled the door shut behind me as I went out. I didn't even realize what I'd done until I'd come back and tried to get in, turning the doorknob left and right.

I was locked out!

Other Apple Paperbacks you will enjoy:

Going on Twelve
by Candice F. Ransom

Eat Your Heart Out, Victoria Chubb
by Joyce Hunt

Living with Dad
by Lynn Zednick

My Sister, the Creep
by Candice F. Ransom

THE
LATCHKEY KIDS

CAROL STANLEY

AN
APPLE
PAPERBACK

SCHOLASTIC INC.
New York Toronto London Auckland Sydney

For Erin and Caitlin

ISBN 0-590-43188-9

12 11 10 9 8 7 6 5 4 3 2 1   1 2 3 4 5 6/9

Printed in the U.S.A.   40

First Scholastic printing, February 1991

1

Whirrrrrrrrrrrrr went my mother's drill. I could hear it from the other room even with my Walkman turned way up. I had a Madonna tape in, so it was kind of like listening to "Madonna Goes to the Dentist."

The dentist is my mom. Barbara Scott, the Friendly Dentist. That's what it says on the office door. She's very painless and sensitive and specializes in people who, if you gave them a choice of going in front of a firing squad or getting into a dentist's chair, they would have a tough decision.

You should see her waiting room when it's full of all these nervous jervouses. If you popped a balloon, they'd go through the ceiling. My mom calms them right down, though. Then she drills their teeth.

That's what she was doing on the other side of the door while I was listening to Madonna. This guy had come in after the regular patients. He

1

was an emergency. When he came through the door, he was holding one side of his face the way people do when they've got a tooth that's in mortal agony. But you could see that at the same time he was scared to death to let anybody touch it. This is where my mom is great.

"Wayne Sneed?" she asked, looking at the folder I'd made up when he called. He was a big guy. Very tall and rugged-looking, with a kind of pie face. Plaid shirt and jeans. You'd think he was a lumberjack except we were in the middle of Chicago where there aren't too many forests that need to be cut down.

"Come in, Wayne," my mom said, reaching up and putting a comforting-type hand on his giant shoulder. She had to reach way up to do this. My mom is kind of short, unlike me. Actually, we don't look much alike at all. I'm tall and thin ("willowy" my mom calls it) with long dark brown hair I pull back in a ponytail most of the time. My eyes are brown, too — real dark. Sometimes when I look in the mirror, I can't see quite where the pupil leaves off and the brown part starts. My mom's eyes are a light gray, and her hair's light, too — brown but on the verge of blonde. Sometimes when we first meet people, they don't even guess we're mother and daughter.

I look much more like my dad is the thing, only he's not around anymore for people to compare us. He died in a car accident when I was only five.

2

Sometimes I can hardly remember him, and then other times, all of a sudden some supersharp memory about him will flash into my mind — like the time he took me to Great America Amusement Park — and it'll seem like the accident just happened, like he was still alive yesterday. And then I get tears in my eyes.

I shook my head to shake away the sad thoughts while I watched my mother take Wayne back into her treatment room. She was using what I call her "calming voice" on him. It's sort of like elevator music, only coming out of a person. She asked him, "What seems to be the problem?"

"Mmmrph. Mmmfffremm," I could hear Wayne say.

"Ah," my mom said, as if she understood. Maybe she did. I think dentists take a course in dental school that teaches them to understand people with toothaches or with those little suction tubes in their mouths.

While she was fixing Wayne's cavity, I went back to doing my job. Every Saturday afternoon I straighten up all the magazines in the waiting room, then I organize the toothbrushes and floss and rubber tips and toothpaste samples in the reception desk. Then I put all of that week's patient files back into the file cabinets. This has to be done alphabetically. No problem, though, because I am a great alphabetizer.

Then I address all the patient reminder cards.

They have a little cartoon character on the back who's saying "Tooth or Consequences!" Unless you remind them, most people completely forget it's time for their dentist appointment. (Big surprise, eh?)

I love my job. It's easy, and I get ten dollars every Saturday. (This also includes my allowance.) Plus I like helping my mother out. And when she's done with the last patient, we hang the little clock sign on the door, setting it to show she'll be back Monday at nine A.M. Then we zip out to have some fun.

Not this Saturday, though. This Saturday she was taking what seemed to be an *incredibly* long time with Wayne Sneed. I could hear her in there telling him how to brush and how to floss. Setting up a whole dental program for him. Then asking him a bunch of personal questions.

"How's your family's dental health?"

Wayne said he didn't really have a family. He had a wife once, but now he was divorced.

Then he was asking her, "Is your husband a dentist, too?"

"He was," my mom said. "I'm a widow."

It was about then that I began to "get it" about my mom and Wayne. They weren't really talking about dental hygiene. They were getting to know each other. I am incredibly good at figuring these things out.

"And this is my daughter, Victoria," my mom

said as she and Wayne came out of the examination room. "But she prefers to be called Tory."

Wayne looked at me like I was only *kind of* there and said, "Hi," while he shook my hand. Then he focused a little more. "How old are you?"

I turned off my Walkman, to be polite.

"Eleven. I'm in the sixth grade. I go to Morris School." I don't know why I was telling him all this. Sometimes I'm just trying to be nice and I realize I'm running on and the person I'm talking to isn't even that interested.

That's what happened then. Wayne turned away from me and said to my mom, "Big for her age, isn't she?"

This is the one thing I most hate for adults to say about me. It's bad enough that I'm taller than every boy in my class except Howard Leyton. On top of this, I have to put up with kids asking me "How's the weather up there?" and other brilliant, witty comments. And then on top of *that*, adults say things like this, as if I'm not standing right there listening.

"She's just shot up like a weed this past year," my mom said, patting me on the head like growing was an accomplishment.

Then Wayne rubbed his jaw and said, "I don't know how to thank you." He meant about his tooth.

"Tell me that again when your novocaine wears off," my mother said in this low, laughing voice.

"I just might do that," Wayne said, meaning he *might* call, but my mom knew and even I knew he was *for sure* going to call. Sometimes I think romance is just too sickening. I can't imagine myself getting romantic with anyone if it would mean looking at him in the flirty way my mom was looking at Wayne.

"So," my mother said when we were out in the park later, flying our latest kite. "What do you think of him?"

"Who?" I said, even though I knew.

"Wayne."

"His hands are clammy. When he shook mine I almost barfed."

"Come on. He'd just had a major filling. Cut the poor guy some slack."

We fly kites a lot on Saturdays when the weather's nice, even in the fall like now. My mother is a great kite flyer (and kite maker!). Sometimes we run into one of her patients out in the park and they're always so surprised to see her running around like a madwoman, trailing a kite behind her. What do they think — that dentists just hang around their offices in their free time, worrying about the cavities of the world?

We'd gotten this new kite up, and now we were just lying side by side on this little rise of grass by the lake. The kite was red and green and high out over the water in a clear blue sky. It was quite a sight.

6

"We have a neat life," I told my mom because that's exactly what I was feeling at the moment. Plus I like to show her I appreciate her. I know it's hard for her, working and being my only parent and all.

"Why do you say we have a neat life?" she asked. "Because when people tell us to 'go fly a kite' we don't mind at all?" She loves to make dumb jokes.

"No," I said. "Because everything we do is fun. And we're a good team. I get to help you out. I think your files would be a big mess without me and you'd lose all your patients."

"Probably," she said. She was humoring me, I could tell, but I didn't really care. I knew I was right. I don't know what my mom *would* do without me.

I closed my eyes, basking in what a perfect moment it was, but, almost immediately, this perfection was interrupted by a big glop of something falling on my forehead. I opened my eyes. I saw it was Karen White, leaning over me with this big double-dip ice cream cone. She's supposed to be my best friend, but as you can see, she is not exactly Princess Di in the manners department.

She doesn't look like Di either. She tries to look wild. For instance, she has three earrings in one ear and wears her hair crimped and long so it's always tangled-looking. She'd like to look even wilder. Once she used a home kit of black dye on her light brown hair, but her mother made her wash it seven times until all the black was out.

"Hey!" I said to her. "Watch where you're dripping!"

"But it's your favorite — Rocky Road."

I sat up and wiped the ice cream off with a finger and licked it.

"Okay then, give me a bite," I said to her and she handed it over as she sat down next to us. She knows we come out here on Saturdays, and so she usually rides her bike over to find us.

"Hi, Karen," my mother said. "You want to take the kite for a while? I'll hold your ice cream for you." She was eyeing Karen's cone with an "I want it" look.

"No you don't!" Karen said, whisking her cone away. "You two are vultures. No one with ice cream is safe around you. And a dentist, too! Doctor Scott, do you really think you should let people see you eating something with so much decay-producing sugar in it?"

My mom had to laugh. She always thinks Karen is funny. But she also thinks Karen is "a pre-teen terror." Which I suppose she is, sort of. Part of how parents think about Karen, why she has this big "reputation," is on account of how she looks. Plus she's in trouble at school a lot, and once she got caught by security guards at the mall. She was dropping water balloons from the top level down onto the heads of people eating at the Pizza Patio on the main floor. Another time she ran away from home and then snuck back up a ladder into her room while everyone was still looking for her. A lot of this, I think, is to get her mother's goat. They don't get along.

I guess my mom's worried that Karen will try to get me into her act, but Karen doesn't. She knows I'm the opposite kind of person from her. I'm not a goody-goody or anything. I just like to keep a low profile, not get demerits at school, and keep my grades in the B range.

When she was finished with her cone, Karen took over the kite flying for a while and the three of us just sort of spaced out lazily through the rest of the afternoon. Karen and I gossiped about kids in our class, and about our teacher, Ms. Randazzo, who — we think — is secretly dating Mr. Thorpe, the assistant principal. Meanwhile my mom took a little snooze. It was very peaceful and everything seemed so perfect that I totally forgot about Wayne, until we got home and there was a message from him on the answering machine (already!).

"Hi," he said. "Well, my mouth is unfrozen now and it doesn't feel too bad. I think by Saturday night I ought to be up to eating a nice dinner out. Do you think you might like to join me? Uh, and of course Vicki can come along, too, if you'd like."

9

"Vicki!" I squealed. "Give me a break."

"I think he meant 'icky,' " my mom said, teasing me.

"Very funny," I said in my least amused voice, then I asked her. "You're not going to go, are you?"

"Oh, I don't know," she said. "Maybe." Which I knew meant "yes."

Argh, I thought. Wayne and my mom liked each other. Which probably meant he was going to start hanging out at our house and taking my mom out on dates, and pretty soon they'd be taking skiing vacations in Colorado. Then they'd be announcing their engagement and getting married and before I knew it, Wayne would be my new stepfather and I'd be stuck with him for the rest of my life. Yikes!

"Wait a minute," I told myself when I realized how many conclusions I'd just jumped to. When I want to, I can really get on a roll. Maybe Wayne would come over once and my mother would decide he was a pie-faced lumberjack who was way too stuffy to be her boyfriend, and that would be the end of that.

Wishful thinking.

2

"**H**ey, Nell!" I called out as I came in the back door of my house after school on Monday and threw my knapsack on the kitchen counter. Nell McBride is my after-school sitter. She stays with me until my mom gets home about six.

"I'm down here!" came her high-pitched voice, sounding more like a young girl than the older woman she really is. "In the basement. I'm checking our mushrooms."

I ran down the stairs to see. These mushrooms were our latest money-making scheme (after our failure at being sweepstakes winners, which we worked at for about six months). We got the mushroom-growing kit through an ad in the back of one of my comic books. Supposedly these mushrooms — a special Italian kind — were going to make me and Nell millions in our spare time — when we got a big enough crop. This part we learned from the booklet that came with the kit — "Mushroom Marketing." So far though, we only had three puny-looking sprouts coming out of the small plastic tray that had come in the mail.

"Four," Nell said, pointing to a new sprout. She had to bend way over to get a closer look. Nell's taller than me, which I like. She's taller than my mom, taller than almost everyone. And she doesn't seem to mind it a bit. She says she thinks it's just that other people are a little on the short side. She has this kind of great attitude about a lot of things. It makes her fun to hang out with. She's been my sitter for three years now, but I know her so well I really can't remember a time when I didn't know her.

She's not strict at all. We've only had one fight the whole time she's been my sitter. It was last year when I found two cans of purple paint in the attic and wanted to paint my bedroom. Later, of course, I was glad she stopped me, but that day I was furious with her.

We both thoroughly inspected the dirt in the mushroom tray for any more signs of new growth. Then she turned to me and asked, "What did the girl mushroom say to the boy mushroom on their first date?"

I could tell from how she said it that this was a riddle. Nell loves riddles. I pretend they're beneath me, but secretly, I like them, too.

"I don't know, Nell," I said in — you know — that phony riddle voice. What *did* the girl mushroom say to the boy mushroom?"

"She said, 'Gee, you're a *fun guy*.' Get it? *Fungi?*"

"I get it, Nell," I said, "but it's a pretty dumb riddle."

"Then why are you giggling?"

She had me there.

"Let's go upstairs and I'll fix us some party sandwiches," she said. Nell's party sandwiches are great. They are a regular sandwich — usually cream cheese and cucumber slices on white bread — but then she trims off the crusts and cuts the rest into four little triangles and serves them on a plate with pickle slices.

"Then can we play Clue?" I asked. She's been teaching me what she calls "Power Clue," which is a way to win by second-guessing what everyone else is holding in their hands of cards.

"No, today I have to tell you something."

I could tell from the way she said this that it was something bad.

"It's something bad, isn't it?" I asked. No sense beating around the bush.

"It's something *both* good and bad," she said.

When we were up in the kitchen — me sitting at the table, her fixing the sandwiches — she dropped the bomb. "I'm going to California soon. To help my daughter. She's having another baby. This makes four little ones she's got at home, and she's tearing her hair out."

"California?" I said, hoping I hadn't heard right.

13

"That's right. San Diego," Nell said.

"But what about me?!" I said. I knew I was wailing like a three-year-old, but I didn't care.

Nell turned to me and gave me the saddest look. "Don't think I haven't given this a lot of hard thought. You know how much I love you — even though you don't properly appreciate my jokes. But really, Tory, I just have to go. Mary Beth needs me to help out, and it's a chance to be part of my family again."

"But you're part of *our* family!" I said, still wailing.

"Yes," Nell said in a calm, reasonable voice. "For three hours a day, five days a week. But then I go home to my little apartment and sometimes I'm quite lonely."

I hadn't thought about this. To tell the truth, I guess I hadn't thought much about what Nell did when she wasn't sitting with me. Sometimes I think I'm an extremely selfish person. It's one of my faults I'm working on. And so I stopped wailing then and told her I agreed it was a good idea for her and her daughter, but that I would really miss her.

"When will you come back?"

"I'm not sure. I'll have to write you when I get there," she said, running her hand through my hair. She loves my hair, says it's my "crowning glory." I didn't used to think much about it one way or the other, but she's made me kind of proud of it. Nell has given me a lot of confidence over these past few years. She makes me feel like I'm a special person. I guess what I'm saying is that she's been more than just a baby-sitter to me. She's not my mom and she's not my grandmother and she's not a friend like Karen exactly. She's more like an aunt to me — the great kind of fun aunt you sometimes see in movies, the ones who take their nieces and nephews off on great adventures and are real characters.

I felt a tear sliding down each of my cheeks. I rubbed my eyes and sniffled and took the tissue she held out to me. I blew my nose a little, then let her give me one of her big hugs while she patted me on the back. She does this — treats me kind of like a baby — when I get upset.

"Mom'll never find a sitter for me as good as you," I muttered into her shoulder.

"Oh, I don't think she's going to get you a sitter from now on," Nell said.

"You guys have already discussed all this?"

"A bit."

"The kid is always the last to know," I said, discouraged. "Why don't I ever get let in on any of the big decisions?" Then I grasped the full meaning of Nell's words. "What do you mean she's not getting me another sitter?"

"She's found an after-school program that sounds good. Happy Hours, I think it's called."

I immediately got on the phone to Karen and

told her all the terrible news of the afternoon.

"I can't believe Nell would leave you," she said. "Do you think she really doesn't care about you all that much?" At school, they call Karen the Tactless Wonder.

"She's got to help her daughter," I tried to explain.

"Do you know who your new sitter's going to be?" she asked me.

"Supposedly I'm going to go to some after-school program. It's called Happy Hours."

"Oh, no!" she shouted into the phone so loud I had to yank the receiver away from my ear. "Alice Fox used to go there. She says all the kids call it Sappy Hours. It's so drippy no one can stand it. It's so boring it's like watching paint dry. It's — "

"Uh, thanks, Karen," I interrupted. "You know how to cheer up a friend in her moment of need."

"Uh-oh," she said. Then there was this long pause before she added, "Maybe it's not so bad. I think I heard Donna Millman say it wasn't too bad."

"Karen. Donna is a barely functioning life-form. Donna makes Popsicle stick placemats for a hobby. If the best *she* can say is that it's *not too bad* — "

I couldn't even finish the sentence. I couldn't stand to think one more thought about Happy Hours. I was just going to have to talk my mother out of sending me there.

I waited until dinner. We'd ordered a pizza and while we were waiting for it to come, my mom fixed a salad. I hiked myself up on the counter next to her and said:

"Nell told me she's leaving."

"Are you sad?"

"Oh, Mom, you know how close Nell and I are."

"I know. That's why I asked *her* to tell you herself."

"Why is it that when there's somebody you really love and feel close to, they always go away."

"What do you . . . ?" my mom asked, then she understood. "Oh, you mean your dad."

I nodded and neither of us said anything for a little while. I guess we were both thinking our own different thoughts on the same subject.

"It doesn't *always* happen that way," she said finally. "And you can't let it make you afraid to get close to someone again. You'll miss Nell, I know, but you have to go on. Even if she wasn't moving, you wouldn't have needed a sitter forever. In fact, I don't think you really need one now."

"I know," I said. "Nell told me you're sending me to some horrible place. Karen says kids die from boredom there. *60 Minutes* is doing a whole show on it."

This got a smile out of her, but it didn't change her mind.

"I don't think Karen's exactly a reliable opinion

17

on what's fun. Karen really needs Las Vegas, or a roller coaster ride to match her energy level. At least a missile launch. Freda Graff has run Happy Hours for years. I've heard she has a nice crafts program, and a little choral group."

I felt myself going into what my mother calls the "whining mode." I couldn't help it, though.

"But I *hate* crafts. And I'm a *terrible* singer."

She scooped up the little tomato wedges she'd just cut up and kind of half dumped/half threw them into a big plastic bowl. I could tell she was getting exasperated with me.

"I guess I *could* get another sitter," she said and sighed. Suddenly I felt awful for being such a big problem for my mom just because I wasn't old enough to stay by myself for a couple of measly hours in the afternoon.

Then I thought — but wait! I'm eleven now. I'm in sixth grade, just one step down from junior high school, which is practically like high school. Maybe I *am* old enough. I tried the idea out on my mom.

"Why can't you just let me stay home by myself until you get here? I could do my homework and my science project. You know how responsible I am. I promise I wouldn't smoke cigars or let any hordes of wild elephants come tromping through the house."

She reached over and tickled me, and said, "You are such a loony girl. Are you sure you're really

18

my daughter? Maybe there was a mix-up at the hospital." But she was laughing when she said it.

The doorbell rang.

"Pizza time!" I shouted, and took her wallet and ran out of the kitchen, heading for the front door, tripping over Calvin and Agnes, our cats, who smelled pizza in the air and so were also making a beeline for the door.

I paid the pizza man and brought the box back (I love how the bottom of pizza boxes are always warm), put it on the kitchen table, and opened it to inhale the steam. My mom brought over plates and napkins and juice and our salad.

"So what about it?" I said, not wanting her to lose track of our conversation. "Can I try staying here by myself?"

"Oh, I don't know, Tory. Maybe if it was just *you*. But there are so many negative influences around these days."

"You mean Karen, don't you?" I asked. "Mom. I am not under her influence. And besides, she's not that bad!"

"Then how come I saw her on a WANTED poster at the Post Office?"

"Ha-ha," I said.

"Tory. Let's compromise. Give Happy Hours a fair try. If you don't like it, we'll go to Plan B."

"What's Plan B?"

"That's the beauty of Plan A. Having one means you don't have to have a Plan B in mind yet."

I had to laugh at this. "Okay," I said. I knew we hadn't really settled anything, but I felt better just not being on the other side of a fence from my mother. That always makes me feel sad. I still didn't want to go to "Sappy Hours," but I could give it a try. And for now at least, there was harmony in our family of two.

For about two seconds. Then my mom said in her way-too-casual voice, which she always uses when she's trying to slip something past me:

"Oh, I don't know if I mentioned this to you, but I called Wayne back about his dinner invitation."

"Oh, Mom! I don't have to go, do I?"

"Of course not. It'd be great if you did, but if you'd rather go to Karen's or something — "

"Oh, I really would," I said, crossing my fingers behind my back, making a wish that she wouldn't already be busy that night.

"Please, Tory," she said. I guess she saw that I was looking a little upset. "Nobody's going to come in here and change what we've got. You are the absolutely Number One person in my book."

I didn't say anything. I just listened as she went on.

"So I can go to dinner with Wayne Sneed, or *we* can go to dinner with him, and our world won't tip on its axis. Maybe the three of us would even have a good time."

Personally I thought the likelihood of that was

about as great as a blizzard happening that weekend — it was only late September. But I knew I should be nicer to my mom about this, and so I said, "Well, if Karen's busy, I'll definitely come along." I tried to sound casual, but inside I was dying to get to the phone to make sure Karen wasn't busy Saturday. If she was, I'd have to offer her a large hunk of my allowance savings to get her un-busy. I'm not sure why, but the idea of going along with my mother on her first date with this guy gave me the willies.

"Karen!" I said, shouting and whispering at the same time into the receiver. "Can I come over to your house on Saturday night? You've just got to do this for me. I'll be forever in your debt if you do. If a giant grizzly bear comes and attacks us, I'll fight him so you can get away — "

"Tory — "

"I'll give you all my Michael Jackson tapes."

"Tory — "

"Yeah?"

"It's fine. I'm not going anywhere Saturday. Sleep over if you want. We can watch *Shock Theater*."

"Oh," I said. "Great. Karen, you're the best friend ever."

"Why do I get the feeling I'm not getting the whole story here?" she asked as my mom started coming up the stairs, and I hung up.

3

We live in an old two-story frame house. It's not very big and not at all glamorous inside, nothing like you'd see in a decorating magazine. But it's cozy. And the best part of the whole house is my room. It's upstairs in the back, and overlooks our rose garden. In the summer, I have the nicest view you could imagine, and when I wake up in the morning, I can already smell the roses as they open up to the sun. But it was late fall now, and the bushes were bare. They looked like gnarled clumps of twigs. Plus, this was an especially gray day — matching my mood exactly. It was Friday — Nell's last day.

It was weird. You'd think I'd want to spend as much time with her as I could. Instead, I'd been sitting up there in my room since I came home from school. I had my desk chair pulled up to the window and my elbows propped on the sill, looking out at the remains of last summer's garden.

I guess I was just so sad about Nell leaving that

I didn't really want to see her. It was as if she were already gone in my mind. If I stayed up there I could pretend she was gone, instead of hanging out with her, being miserable because we'd both know it was our last afternoon together. At least our last afternoon together for a long while.

But then I heard her shouting up to me.

"Tory! Come on down! This is important!"

I could tell from the laughter behind her voice, though, that it was something very *not* important, that she had something silly up her sleeve.

She was sitting at the kitchen table. In front of her, she had a phony-baloney certificate she'd just finished coloring and filling out.

"What's that?" I asked.

"The deed to the mushroom farm," she said. "I'm turning the whole corporation over to you."

"I'm speechless," I said, trying to match her mock sincerity.

"Oh, no!" she said, "and I was just going to ask you to make a speech. Will you at least shake on the deal with me?" she asked, holding out her hand to me.

But the handshake turned into one of her great big hugs and before you knew it, we were both in tears.

"I could never like another sitter as well as you," I said into her shoulder. "So it's probably good Mom didn't even try."

* * *

23

Still, I couldn't say I was looking forward to *not* having another sitter, because that meant one thing — Happy Hours.

I talked with Karen about it some more on Saturday. She came by in the morning to help me get Calvin and Agnes to the vet for their booster shots. This is a two-person job at least. You really need about ten people just to trap those cats in their carriers. As soon as they see their cases come down off the closet shelf, they turn from peaceful little pets into *flying demon fur balls*!

We finally captured the cats by waving an open can of sardines through the air. Then, when they poked their noses out, we grabbed them and stuffed them inside the cases and slammed the doors shut. We carried them over to Dr. Farnsworth's office, trying to not jiggle the carriers around too much as we walked.

"You don't seem like your happy old self," Karen said. "What's the prob?"

"My list of worries is growing longer by the day," I told her. "First there's Happy Hours."

"Maybe it won't be *so* bad," she said lamely.

"Yeah," I said sarcastically. "Maybe I'll really get into making Popsicle stick pot rests."

"Why can't you just stay home by yourself? I practically do. I mean, half the time when my mom's supposed to be home with me, she's really off at the grocery store, or taking Eric to the park or something."

24

"I know," I said and sighed. "I was thinking about that. But you know my mom's going to say that's different, that your mother is never very far away."

All of a sudden Karen laughed. She has the wildest laugh.

"What's so funny?" I asked.

"Well it's just pretty weird. My parents leave *me* — the craziest kid east of the Pecos — home alone all the time, and your mother won't leave you — the World's Most Reponsible Kid — home alone at all."

"I'm just responsible compared to you," I said.

"Thanks," Karen said and stuck her tongue out at me. Sometimes we act more seven than eleven.

"Hey," I said to her. "You didn't forget about tonight, did you?"

"You mean providing you an escape from the *Love Boat*? Boy, I love when your mother gets a boyfriend. They're usually such turkeys!" She let out with her maniac laugh again.

"You think it's funny because it's not *your* mother. None of these guys could turn into your instant father."

"Oh, your mom's not going to rush into anything. She hasn't married any of these gobblers yet."

"You're probably right," I said, telling myself I was being silly. Still, it seemed like too much was changing in my life all at once — Nell leaving,

Wayne arriving, and my having to go to an after-school program — and I didn't have a choice in any of it.

We'd gotten to Dr. Farnsworth's office by now and set the cat carriers down on the floor of the waiting room. I looked inside mine and saw Agnes huddled way at the back, looking small and scared and depressed about her immediate future.

"I know just how you feel," I told her through the little grate.

Wayne looked kind of different when he showed up at our house at exactly eight o'clock on the dot. I was just walking through the downstairs hall-way when the doorbell rang. He was so on time I didn't think it could possibly be him (adults are *always* late), and so I figured it must be Karen wondering where I was, or something. I ran and threw open the door and there was Wayne, doing a little last-minute sprucing up. He was using the brass on the lamp outside as a mirror, peering into it like a madman to comb his hair. He doesn't have too much on top, so he was trying to spread it around to make it look like there was more than there was.

I could tell he was just dying of embarrassment, getting caught like that. Even though I didn't like him, I felt bad. I hate being embarrassed myself. And so I tried to be nice.

"It looks good now," I said, nodding toward the top of his head.

This just made him turn a deeper shade of red. Beet, to be exact.

"Uh, thanks, Vicki," he said.

I winced. I don't much like it when anybody calls me Victoria, but I positively hate it when they call me Vicki.

"It's Tory," I said.

"Oh," he said. "Sorry. Here, I brought some cheese and crackers. A little appetizer before your Mom and I go out." He handed me a little white paper sack. "You can have some, too."

"Oh," I said. "Thanks. Come on in. My mom had an emergency and didn't get back here until late. She's upstairs getting ready now. I'm supposed to talk to you. It shouldn't be long." This was what my mom calls a "polite social lie." I knew she'd just gotten into the shower. Which meant I had quite a while ahead of me to entertain Wayne alone.

I'd almost gotten out of this entirely. I had just been putting on my coat to go to Karen's, when my mom came rushing in through the back door and told me I had to stay and help her out.

I didn't feel up to this at all. I'm not sure why. Usually I'm pretty good at talking with people. Not just other kids, but teachers, my mom's friends. But I knew I was going to have trouble making small talk with Wayne. He was so stony, standing there with his hands jammed in his pockets. He looked like a giant rock.

"Uh," I said brilliantly, "I'll just go put your cheese and crackers on a plate or something."

He followed me into the kitchen, stiffly, the way a rock would walk if rocks walked.

I took out the cheese — a block of cheddar — and the package of saltines and arranged them on a little plate. I asked him if he wanted anything to drink and he said a soda would be nice, and so I went to the refrigerator. While I had my head in there, poking around to come up with a ginger ale, I heard Wayne clearing his throat behind me. That's how I knew he was about to say something.

"So," he said, "how are we doing at school?"

At first I thought he must mean him and me, and I thought, But you're way too old to go to my school. And then I realized he just meant me. How was *I* doing.

"Fine," I said. What I was really thinking, though, was, Argh. It was clear Wayne hardly ever talked to kids. Otherwise he'd know we hate this question. And that we doubly hate grown-ups who talk to us as though we're in nursery school.

"And we're in what grade now?" He kept going.

"Sixth," I said to be polite, even though he'd already asked me this the other day. "Would you like to come in the living room and wait for my mother there?" If I didn't change the subject, he was for sure going to ask me if I had a boyfriend. That's what adults like him always ask after they ask how you're doing at school. Even if you're five, they ask you this.

When we got into the living room, I took the wing chair across the room. He sat down on the sofa. Then he leaned forward, like he was the detective and I was the main suspect in his case.

"Are you a good student?"

"Pretty good," I said. This was a tricky question. The truth is that I'm an okay student, but just barely. I get mostly B's, but some C's, and I got a D in history last year mainly because I couldn't stand all the memorizing. Mom would like me to do a little better. I'd like that, too, actually, but I guess not enough to really knuckle down. Anyway, I didn't want to talk about all this with Wayne.

He took one of his crackers and sliced off a neat piece of cheese that fit on top of the cracker almost exactly. He ate it in small bites so he wouldn't get any crumbs on his shirt.

"I think kids today take it way too easy," was the next thing he said. "American kids, anyway. In Japan they have to study all the time. Even during their vacations."

"Uh," I said. "Do you have any kids of your

own?" What rotten luck for them, having Wayne as a dad. He probably made them study on their vacation to Disney World.

But it turned out he didn't have any kids.

"Not yet anyway," he said with what I thought was a significant look, and I thought, Oh, no. He's planning on marrying Mom and being my stepfather! Then I had an even worse thought. He's planning on marrying Mom and having a baby of their own. A creepy little kid who'll look just like Wayne and they'll shower all their attention on him and send him to Japanese schools where he'll become a genius.

Wayne was looking at his watch and then toward the stairs. He and I were clearly having the same thought — where was my mother!?

"I'll just go see if she's ready," I said and practically bolted out of the room.

When I got to the upstairs hallway, I couldn't believe my ears. My mom was still in the shower. I could hear the running water and hear her singing "Hey, Jude."

I pounded on the door.

"Hey, Tore," she sang back at me, "don't be afra-a-a-id. Take a sad song . . ."

I pushed against the bathroom door and shouted in, "Please, Mom, hurry. I'm running out of stuff to talk about with him."

She stuck her head out and said blithely, "I'm

sure you're doing great. What do you think I should wear?"

"Your tan pants and the navy sweater." This was my favorite outfit of hers.

"Is he an interesting conversationalist?" she asked, meaning Wayne.

"I wouldn't say he's David Letterman. Come on, you can find out for yourself."

"Oh, all right. Toss me that towel."

I gritted my teeth and headed back downstairs. Wayne was still sitting on the sofa, but he'd eaten almost all the cheese and had gotten himself another glass of soda. He looked up and focused in on me again.

"You know, you slouch."

"I know." People have been telling me this ever since I started getting tall last year. Maybe I slouch so I won't look so tall.

"I used to slouch myself," he said. It was the first time since he'd gotten here that I felt like he was talking like a real person instead of like a serious PBS show on child raising. I was almost starting to relax a little, when he went on. "My mother got me this kind of harness. A posture support brace that *made* me stand up straight. I'll bet I still have it around somewhere. I could bring it by next time. It might help you with your problem. I could talk with your mother about it."

Back brace! I thought. This guy was worse than I thought — a real menace to the nice easygoing lifestyle my mom and I enjoyed. I didn't even want to think of all the ideas he could put into my mother's head about raising me more strictly.

Wayne was getting impatient for her to come down, I could tell. He was looking at his watch for about the fifth time since he'd arrived. And just about then (mercifully!) I heard her footsteps coming down the stairs and there she was.

I heard Wayne let out a little sigh, which I took to mean he liked how my mom looked. When she gets fixed up she's really pretty, I think, and tonight, in addition to her nicest outfit, she had put on light makeup and moussed her hair so it scattered around her face in this soft way.

"Hello, Wayne," she said. "Sorry I'm late, but I guess you of all people would understand a dental emergency. I hope you two've been having a good time without me."

Wayne kind of grunted at this, and I went to the closet to get my jacket and overnight backpack out of the hall closet.

"Uh, well, Karen's waiting for me to have dinner, so I'd better get going," I said. "It was nice talking with you, Wayne," I lied.

"Be back here first thing in the morning!" I heard my mother shouting from the other side of the front dooor, which I'd just pulled shut behind me. I dashed past the four houses between my house and Karen's, and when she answered the door, I dropped to my knees before her in mock gratitude.

"Oh, thank you, most wonderful friend," I said, taking her hand and kissing her ring as if she were a king. We can get pretty silly sometimes, I'll admit. "You've saved me from a fate worse than midterms — a night of Wayne Sneed."

"Is he really that bad?" Karen asked me a little later after we'd made our "dinner" — a big bowl of microwave popcorn — and snuggled into side-by-side sleeping bags in front of the TV. Her parents and brother were out shopping, so we could talk freely.

"Well, let's put it this way," I told her about Wayne. "In the half hour I had to talk to him, he'd already planned out most of the rest of my kidhood and was probably about to move onto my teenage years. If I'd gone to dinner with them, by dessert, I'm sure he would've had suggestions about my wedding and how many children I should have. Oh, and he's also very helpful about improving my posture."

"Oh, boy," Karen said. "This guy *does* sound worse than the rest. But your mom will see that. He probably won't be around for long."

I nodded my head, hoping she was right.

"We'll ask the crystal ball later," she said. Karen has this great crystal ball. It's like one of those shaky snowy things you turn upside down and then right side up again and watch the snow blow around inside. Only in this one, there's a little disk that spins around, too, and lands with either YES or NO facing up as an answer to your questions.

When I asked "Is Wayne going to be around in my life for a while," it said, YES.

"Argh," I said to Karen. But by the next day I didn't have any more time to brood about Wayne. He got completely forced out by my brooding about Happy Hours.

4

Monday morning I thought of trying to talk my mom out of sending me to Happy Hours, but then I thought better of it. She was in too good a mood for me to make a dent with any complaining. She was humming around the kitchen, making me pancakes for breakfast, which she never does on weekdays. She'd been happy and humming off and on all day Sunday, too. This had to do with a certain pie-faced lumberjacky-looking guy.

"My mom's got a mild case of Wayne-itis," I told Karen at lunch in the cafeteria. "She's way too blissed out to care that I'm being shipped off to Sappy Hours."

Karen was a *big* help. She sat across from me sipping her chocolate milk through a straw poked into the carton and said, "Boy, am I glad I've got a regular family with two parents and a mother who stays home so I don't have to go wandering around looking for someone to take me in after school."

"Thanks a lot," I said sarcastically. Actually, I'm really proud of my mom — being a dentist and all — but there are moments when I do selfishly wish she didn't have to work and could just stay at home and be there whenever I needed to be taken care of. A bright light bulb clicked on in my head. Karen's mother *was* home all the time!

"Hey," I said to Karen. "Maybe I could stay at your house after school. Maybe your mom wouldn't mind. She thinks I'm such a good influence on you."

"I don't know," Karen said, thinking this over between chocolate sips. "She's always saying she's going to abandon me and Eric outside a convent and run off and join a circus. She thinks we're too much work. I don't know if she'd be crazy about taking on a third kid."

"But you'll ask her," I said.

"Okay, I'll ask," Karen said, but I could tell she wasn't looking forward to it.

After school, I stood outside watching the other kids getting picked up by their mothers, or riding off on their bikes toward happy homes with moms waiting with platters of fresh-baked cookies. At least that's how I imagined it. I knew I was getting carried away, but I didn't care. Sometimes when I'm sad, I start thinking stuff that makes me even sadder. Just to torture myself, I guess.

On the way to Happy Hours, I walked as slowly as I could, taking little baby steps. The program is held in a church basement a couple of blocks from my school. I went down the church stairs about an inch at a time. When I came through the door, Mrs. Graff came over to meet me. She's a big woman, but flutters like a ballet dancer. I already knew her because she's one of my mom's patients.

"Tory, hello! Welcome to our little group!"

And she wasn't kidding about the "little" part. I was the oldest kid there by four or five years. There were all these six- and seven-year-olds sitting around a long table, playing with clay and finger painting.

"Why don't you sit down here on the end," she suggested.

"Uh, doesn't Donna Millman come here?" I asked. She was a dolt, but at least she was a dolt my age.

"Donna's not with us anymore," Mrs. Graff said. "Which means you can be our new junior counselor!" I knew she was trying to make this sound like a big honor, but I wasn't too excited, if you know what I mean.

Mrs. Graff led me to my place at the end of the table, and as I sat down said to me, "This is our crafts hour. Would you rather work with Play Doh, or finger paints?"

I was too miserable to answer. I just watched with dead eyes as Mrs. Graff slapped a large clump of pink Play Doh in front of me. When she left to help one of the other kids, the little girl next to me tugged at my sleeve. I turned to look at her. She was about five and her nose was running.

"What?" I asked.

She looked at me smugly and said, "I just ate my crayon."

My mom was waiting for me when I got home. She'd forgotten to take off her white dentist's jacket, a sure sign she was distracted. She was sitting in the living room, curled up at one end of the sofa with a book, but when I came into the room she was looking up at me with such a big stare that I knew she hadn't really been reading. She was nervous to know how I was. This made me feel better, somehow.

"So?" she asked. "How'd it go at Happy Hours?"

I had planned to be very cool, to tell her about the whole thing calmly, to explain why the program was just not for me, and to show her why she should consider letting me out of it.

What I did instead, though, was burst out crying. I probably looked like one of those babies in cartoons going "Waaaaa!" I didn't care. I tumbled on top of her on the sofa, still crying like crazy.

"I guess it wasn't too great," she said.

Somehow, in the middle of my crying, this understatement made me start laughing instead. Which got my mom laughing, too, and then she said, "Details. I want all the gory details."

"It wasn't an after-school group. It was a playpen. Here," I said, pulling a squooshed blob out of my jacket pocket. "Here's what I made you today from Play Doh."

I told her how Mrs. Graff passed around cookies and milk, and a couple of kids got into a food fight. "I took their cookies away to stop them. Then we were supposed to roll out our nap rugs. I was only about two feet too long for mine. I was also the only one not sucking my thumb. And then this little kid started sleepwalking and I had to chase him out of the room and bring him back."

"Maybe you could get some baby-sitting skills out of the experience."

"But if I'm ready to be a baby-sitter, why can't I baby-sit myself?" I asked.

One thing about my mother is that she's usually fair. "Let me think about that, will you?"

We went out to dinner, which we do a lot. There's a Thai restaurant just down our street that we like. Actually we like pretty much *any* Thai restaurant and Chicago has a lot of them. They're like Chinese restaurants, only not quite.

We'd just ordered our dinner, when in came one of the weirdest patients my mother has — a woman named Crystal Moonglow. I think she

39

must have made up this name. I mean, I can't really imagine that her parents are Mr. and Mrs. Moonglow. Anyway, you'd notice Crystal in any crowd. She has hair that's about one inch long and bleached almost white, like Annie Lennox. She wears these hoop earrings so big they look more like bracelets. She wears clothes that are cool, but in a unique way — flowing tops and dresses and long scarves around her neck, and sometimes another scarf tied around her head. She teaches meditation at a place she calls "The Peaceful Garden."

She came through the door of Thai Valley all by herself and seemed really happy to see us. She was waving all the way across the restaurant, and then sat down in one of the empty chairs at our table.

"Why don't you join us?" my mother asked, even though Crystal had already done just that.

"Thanks. I'm all by myself tonight, as you see. I could use the company." She settled into her chair with a lot of rearranging of her scarves.

"So, Crystal, how's it going?" my mother said.

"Oh," Crystal said, suddenly looking guilty. "I've been flossing every day, just like you advised."

You can't believe how many people say this when they run into my mother outside the office. It's like they think dentists are part of some dental police force, keeping track of everyone's flossing

and brushing and if they use antiplaque toothpaste. And most of these people — including
Crystal — are such terrible liars. You can tell at
a glance that they have *not* been flossing every
day. My mom's used to this, though. Like with
Crystal, she just nodded and said:

"Great. Keep up the good work."

"What's new with you two? Any big develop-
ments — professional or personal? Crystal likes
to hear all, know all." She has the funniest way
of talking. The thing is, I've never known whether
she means to be funny or not, and so I never know
whether it's okay to laugh.

"Tory and I were just discussing what we're
going to do with her after school. Nell McBride's
out in California, and I can't seem to find a suitable
after-school program. One that would be good for
someone her age."

"The age of someone who's really too old for
after-school programs," I said.

"That's the issue we've been debating," my
mom explained to Crystal.

"Wow!" Crystal said, clapping her hands together. "Is this synchronicity or what?"

"Sync — ?" my mom said.

"Well, the three of us just running into each
other like this. You — looking for just the right
after-school program for a mature, sophisticated,
spiritually inclined girl like Tory. (Spiritually inclined? I thought. Me?) And me — holding a

young people's meditation group from three to five every afternoon.

Oh, no, I thought, seeing what was coming. I looked across the table at my mom. I tried to send desperation signals across to her. But clearly she couldn't think of any way out, either.

"Well, that sounds intriguing, of course, but Tory's never really done any meditating."

"Oh, I think she'd love it once she got into it. It really seems to calm the kids down, gets them to focus. In most cases, they find they study better and get much higher grades."

"Meditation improves *grades*?" I heard my mother saying, and I saw in a flash where I'd be sitting the next day from three to five.

5

I was late getting to Peaceful Garden the next afternoon. Partly I was dragging my feet because I didn't want to go; partly I really couldn't find the place. I guess I thought it would be like a school, with a sign. But it turned out to be just the first floor of Crystal Moonglow's big old house.

There was a small card tacked to the front door.

PLEASE COME IN AND REMOVE YOUR SHOES.

I took off my running shoes, and left them among the large cluster of other shoes — mostly thick sandals — in the front hallway. Then I walked in and looked around. I'd never seen anything quite like this before. It looked like a living room that someone had sucked out with a giant vacuum cleaner. The furniture, carpet, TV set, the pictures on the walls. What was left were pale peach walls and a ceiling hung with odd mobiles made of branches and feathers, and a bare wood floor on which there were about ten sitting kids (a lot of them my age this time).

They all had their legs crossed in this funny way with one foot on top of the other leg. They had their eyes closed and were making funny sounds. Like humming. These noises kind of blended in with the weird music coming from the stereo. I can't really describe this music. It was soft and tingly and reminded me of a cross between forests and spaceships.

Crystal saw me come in and put a finger to her lips to let me know I should be quiet, which I'd already figured out. And then she pointed to a vacant spot on the floor in the back. I tiptoed over and sat down. I took off my jacket, slowly so as not to disturb anyone. Then I tried to imitate the position everyone was sitting in, but I couldn't get my legs folded right. I had to settle for crossing them in the regular old way, the way you sit when you're singing songs in front of a campfire.

I looked up at Crystal, who was now pointing to her eyes and closing them to show me I should do the same thing. So I did.

I listened to the music and everybody chanting around it, but it got more and more boring until I finally got a bright idea of how to liven it up. With a little *real* music — rock music. I quietly took my Walkman out of my backpack, put the headphones over my ears, and switched on a nice blast of Steve Winwood.

The thing about personal stereos, though, is that they really aren't all that personal. You tend to forget, once you're inside them, that just enough sound creeps out to make a buzzing that can be incredibly irritating to the people around you.

I remembered this a little too late — when I felt a hand shaking me gently by the shoulder. I opened my eyes and looked up to see Crystal.

"Tory, you're disrupting everyone."

"Oh, boy. I'm sorry, Crystal," I said.

"You can't have your radio on anyway," she said patiently. "It'll interfere with your meditation."

"Oh," I said in my smallest voice. "Okay." I took off my headphones, stuffed the Walkman back into my knapsack, and smiled up at Crystal apologetically.

"It won't happen again," I told her. "I'll go with the program, give this my best try."

She nodded and patted my head, then walked back to the front of the group and put in a new tape, which sounded exactly like the old tape, and told everyone, "Begin your mantras again."

I didn't know what a mantra was, so I just started humming the most boring song I could think of — "Row, Row, Row Your Boat." The more I hummed, the more peaceful I felt. *Really* peaceful. So incredibly peaceful. And then the boat in the song started me thinking about my mother telling me Wayne had a cottage on Lake

Michigan, outside the city, and that he wanted to take us fishing sometime in his boat. And this led me into a big fantasy with Wayne and me and my mom fishing and Wayne getting pulled in by a huge dolphin on the end of his line, and us not being able to get the boat back to him. I didn't want Wayne to drown — I didn't hate him that much — and so I had a Japanese fishing boat come along and pick him up and take him to Japan forever.

And then all of a sudden I was being arrested by the Coast Guard. Someone had a hand on my shoulder, shaking it.

I opened my eyes. It was Crystal. Uh-oh. This fishing fantasy hadn't been a fantasy at all. It was a dream.

Crystal and I were alone. All the other kids were gone. The spacey music was gone. I realized where my incredible peacefulness had led me — straight into a deep sleep. It looked like I'd napped right through the afternoon.

"Oh, Crystal, I'm so sorry." And I really was. She was such a nice person, and such a believer in meditation, and here I was looking like I didn't care a bit about it. "I think I might just be the wrong personality type for this," I told her, trying to take the blame onto myself.

"Well," Crystal admitted, "I wouldn't say you're my *most* promising student. Maybe you need something to do after school that's a little *less* peaceful. Maybe roller coaster riding, or stock car racing. Dynamiting tunnels through mountains."

She was being nice, kidding around with me this way, but I knew that underneath, she probably wished I'd drop out of the group — leave it in peace.

This was okay with me. I could tell I'd never really get into meditation. But I was sorry I'd goofed up. I didn't want to be a big pain to my mother, but here I was, barely into Plan B, and now I'd have to tell her we needed a Plan C.

As I was putting my shoes back on in the hall-way, I could see that the girl who'd been sitting next to me in the group was still hanging out on the front porch. She was the friendliest-looking person — short, a little chubby, with a mop of curly brown hair, and big glasses.

"I thought I'd wait for you," she said when I came outside.

"Why?"

She shrugged.

"I don't know."

Then she asked which way I was going.

"I live on Buckingham," I told her.

"That's right by me. I live on Elaine Place. Want to walk together?"

I said sure. We introduced ourselves.

"I'm Lucy French," she said. "You were really funny in there."

"I thought everyone was probably mad at me."

"Not me. I hate meditation. I just sit there thinking about Jeremy Fuller. He's this guy I'm crazy about. He's thirteen. I'm twelve so that's not really such a big gap. The big gap is he doesn't know I exist."

I'd never met anyone who talked so fast, or changed subjects so much. I tried to get her back to the one that interested me.

"If you hate meditation, then why are you here?"

"Oh, my parents both work. They don't want to let me be a latchkey kid."

"What's that?"

"That's when you get to keep your own house key and let yourself into your house and you're on your own until your parents get home."

"That's what I want! But what did you call it?"

"Latchkey kid. Some of the kids at my school are latchkey kids. I think it's neat. My mom worries something will go wrong, though, if I'm on my own. I think it's ridiculous. I mean, some of the girls in my class have baby-sitting jobs already. Other people trust them to take care of *their* kids."

"I know," I said dejectedly. "I made the same point to my mom."

"You must be twelve," she said.

"No. Eleven. I'm just tall for my age."

"Oh," Lucy said. "I guess you are." I immediately liked her. I always like people who don't notice or care if I'm tall.

"My mom works down at the Art Institute," she said. "We can go down and she'll pass us in. Want to sometime?"

"Sure!" I said, and we exchanged our phone numbers on little slips of paper. Lucy went to Catholic school, which is why I'd never seen her around Morris, my school. We came to her street first and she turned off and I walked the rest of the way home alone thinking about my funny new friend, and two particular words — latchkey kid.

Now I knew what I wanted to be!

6

"I hate English," Karen said the next day as we were being pushed along by the crowd of kids piling into the cafeteria. "Mr. Eastman handed me back this paper and it's so marked up you can barely see what I wrote in the first place." She showed me.

"Maybe you should just move to France," I suggested. "It's probably not too late. Then you could learn French instead of English. You could move in with a French family, leave yours over here. You'd be rid of Eric. The bad part is you'd have to eat a lot of cheese. French people love cheese." I knew Karen hated it.

"Oh, by the way," she said, changing the subject so I'd stop teasing her. "I asked my mom if you could stay with us after school and she said no. She said one more kid — even one as nice as you — would put her over the edge and they'd have to haul her off to the insane asylum in a straitjacket."

I knew she expected me to be disappointed. So she looked real surprised when I said, "That's okay. I've got another plan. Today my mom's taking the afternoon off. We're going shopping to get me some new shoes and she's going to want to talk about Plan C — what she's going to do with me after school *now*. I know she's already called four other programs, but they were full. So I'm going to pounce on her with *my* Plan C — letting me become a latchkey kid." I kind of liked just saying the words. Latchkey kid. I thought maybe Karen wouldn't know what I was talking about and I could have one up on her. But she just said:

"Oh, yeah. Like the Burris Twins."

"They're Latchkey kids?"

"Uh-huh."

"I think I ought to talk with them in that case," I said.

I spotted for them later out on the playground during recess.

"Hey, Burris!" I shouted, which got both of them to turn around at the same time. Although they are twins and always hanging around with each other, they look very different. That is, they look basically identical, but their styles are opposite. Michael Burris is about the straightest kid I've ever seen. He's the only boy I've ever seen wear a shirt and tie to school. And he always has his red hair neatly combed in place and two pens in his pocket and nice white running shoes. David,

51

on the other hand, has his red hair gelled up in spikes. They've both been in my class since kindergarten, so even though I don't know them well, I've known them forever and so it was easy just asking them all the questions I had.

"Karen tells me you guys are latchkey kids."

"Yeah," David said, and shrugged. "So what?"

"Yes, we are, Tory," Michael said ultrapolitely, pulling a house key out of his pocket — sort of like a visual aid.

I told them I was trying to talk my mom into letting me be one. "Maybe she could call your mom, find out how it works," I said.

"Sure," David said.

"Do you know any other latchkey kids so I could have her call their moms, too?"

David shook his head.

Michael said, "Just Cindy Tompkins, and you might not want your mom calling her house. Cindy *hates* being a latchkey kid. She just wants her mother to quit her job and stay home and bake her tollhouse cookies and play gin rummy with her."

"But you guys like it, right?"

"Oh, yeah," said David. "But there's stuff you've got to know. How to do things around the house yourself. And who to call when there's something you can't figure out."

"We've got a list of emergency numbers a mile

long stuck on the refrigerator door," Michael said.

"Do you have rules?"

"You mean like not burning down the house, or having wild parties, or practicing parachuting off the garage roof?" Michael teased me. "Sure. Of course, most of those rules are for David."

At this, David gave his brother a quick punch in the ribs and the two of them started tumbling all over each other on the playground, fighting and laughing at the same time. I wasn't going to get any more helpful hints out of them just then.

All the way home, I prepared my little speech. I tried to sound sensible and sincere — like those actors who play doctors on TV commercials. I had such a strong picture of this conversation in my mind: me and Mom sitting at the kitchen, me talking and her nodding in agreement that my being a latchkey kid was simply the most practical solution. So I was stunned when I actually came into the kitchen and she wasn't alone. There, sitting in my place at the table was — Wayne!

"Honey," my mom said to me in that musical voice she used when he was around, "Wayne came by to take us to the zoo this afternoon. Isn't that nice?" Wayne sells something — real estate or insurance, I never can remember which — so he can just take off whenever he wants, even afternoons, to come visit. Lucky us.

The worst thing was that I *loved* the zoo and the last person I wanted to spend time there with was Wayne.

But there was no getting out of this. I just dug my fists into my jacket pockets, and tried to smile politely while we all went out to Wayne's car. I was surprised to find that it was a convertible sports car. I got to sit in back in this little place that wasn't really a seat. It was kind of neat, like a cubbyhole with a plastic window.

"Can we put the top down?" I asked him, even though it was pretty cold out. He seemed like such a stuffy guy that I didn't really think he'd say yes in a million years. But he surprised me. He looked like he was thinking it over for a few seconds, then said, "It's okay by me if your mother doesn't mind."

"We'll look pretty odd," she said, laughing a little, "but why not, I guess?"

Wayne buzzed the top down and we drove to the zoo bundled up in our jackets with the heater blasting, but I was happy in a goofy way and I think they were, too. The sky was as sunny as if it was still summer, and it felt kind of like we were cheating the seasons.

Going through the zoo with Wayne wasn't as much fun as going with just my mom. We usually take it pretty casual, just looking at the animals, especially our favorites — a monkey named Chi Chi, and one of the panthers, and the craziest of

54

the mynah birds. We like how they look back, probably thinking we're the poor dumb animals, having to wear heavy clothes and not being able to roar or fly or even swing from branch to branch.

Wayne had more of a "field trip" attitude. He kept telling me all the Latin names of the animals and lecturing me on what they ate and where they came from. But I was still liking him more for putting the top down in the car, and so I pretended I was real interested in his little lectures. I think he was partly trying to make friends with me, partly trying to impress my mother. I guess it worked. When we were in the zoo gift shop, he came up to her with a stuffed lion and was making the lion "bite" her arm. He was going *"grrrr,"* and my mom was giggling, which is *not* her usual style. It was then that I began to see that my mother needed contact with the "opposite sex," as Karen refers to guys. While I was probably more brilliant and witty, she needed an adult companion, too, and Wayne was it.

I felt incredibly grown-up figuring this out. And it even made me feel better about Wayne for a little while — as though he served some purpose in hanging around, aside from just making me miserable. But this little burst of good feeling only lasted a few minutes. Until we were having dinner at this burger place — all three of us — and my mother informed me that Wayne had the solution to my after-school problem.

"Wayne's boss sends his kids to a terrific program," she said as the waitress set little plastic baskets filled with burgers and fries in front of us.

Wayne nodded and squeezed ketchup on his fries. "It's called KidSkills," he told me across the table in his booming voice. "It's very goal-oriented. I don't think you'll be bored there like you were in those other programs." Clearly my mom had been talking to him. For some reason this made me really mad. Plus, I was nervous about this line of talk. Basically you never want adults to think you're bored. They've always got something for you to do that's worse than boring. Cleaning your room, or mowing the lawn, or going through all the rusty cans under the cobwebs in the basement workshop and sorting out the rusty nails by size. Stuff like that.

"Uh, what does goal-oriented mean?" I asked Wayne. I was afraid to ask, and at the same time afraid not to.

"The program tries to prepare kids for a rugged survival existence. Making do with the basics. Foraging for roots and berries, fishing with your bare hands. Making a bed out of pine quills. Knowing how to find your way out of a mountain pass after an avalanche."

"But I live in a big city," I said. "I already have a nice bed and I don't have to forage for breakfast. I just open a box of cereal. And there are no mountains around here, so I don't have to worry about avalanches."

Wayne looked at me as if I'd insulted him in a major way, which I really hadn't meant to do. I was just being logical. My mom tried to smooth things over.

"Honey, where's your sense of adventure? Doesn't it sound like a real challenge?"

"I guess," I said, although I must admit I'm about the biggest softie there is. Playing "Red Rover" is about as much physical challenge as I can stand. The thought of learning all these survival skills sent shivers of fear through me. I was going to be terrible at this stuff and everyone would laugh at me. I didn't want to say this in front of Wayne, though. He already thought I was such a wimp.

"I'm sure you'll love it," my mom chimed in, "once you get there."

"Probably," I said, although I was almost positive I wouldn't.

"It'll toughen you up," Wayne told me. "I hear the final exam is staring down a rattlesnake to make him slither away."

If it was anybody else, I would have been *sure* they were joking, but with Wayne, I couldn't tell. He was turning out to be a different person from who I thought he was at first. But now I wasn't sure exactly what kind of person he really *was*.

7

"Tory?" my mom said, shaking me gently by the shoulder. I sat up and rubbed my eyes. I guess I must have fallen asleep with my face on my arm on the reception desk in her office. "Boy, it's hard to get good help these days," she teased me, pointing to the rag and bottle of furniture polish next to my elbow.

I yawned and said, "Sorry. I was just going to get to this. I don't know what happened."

"An unplanned nap would be my guess," she said and then felt my forehead with her palm. "No fever."

Then she looked closely at me.

"What are these circles under your eyes?" she asked. "Have you been getting enough sleep?"

"I think so. The same as usual. I guess maybe it's not enough now that I'm in school *and* in KidSkills."

"I thought you were enjoying it there," she said.

"You haven't said anything bad about it."

"Yeah, it's great," I lied. I didn't want to seem like the wimp Wayne thought I was, didn't want to give him the satisfaction of seeing me quit.

"Tory Scott," she said, pulling me up by the shoulders and looking me straight in the eye. "You are talking to the person who knows you best in the world. Plus you're a terrible liar, and probably couldn't fool a complete stranger. So, you might as well spill the beans. What's wrong?"

Whenever anybody — a teacher or a friend, but especially my mom — talks to me in that concerned voice filled with kindness, it gets me every time. I just go to pieces and start crying all over the place.

"Oh, Mom!" I bawled. "It's just so hard! We're always setting up tents and I can never remember all the knots we're supposed to use. Then we have to look for kindling and then rub sticks together until we get a spark to light the tinder. Then we build the campfire to warm the water for our bark tea. Then we have to draw water from the stream."

"What's bark tea? And what stream? — I thought this was being held in the park? And why can't you just boil water on a camp stove?"

"Mom, that's the whole point of KidSkills — not to do anything the easy, modern way. We pretend the drinking fountain is the stream. And that we're not in Lincoln Park, but some remote wilderness and that we're a tribe of hunter-gatherers."

"What do you hunt and gather?"

"Well, a lot of the kids gather hot dogs and sodas at the park stands, but that's only when Ranger Jack's looking the other way."

"Do you like him?"

I wiped my eyes. I'd finally stopped crying, and in the same way that my tears had poured out before, words poured out now.

"Not much. He makes us run back and forth on the beach to toughen up our legs. Then we have to climb trees. Then we do push-ups. Then he teaches us how to carry someone away on a litter in case they've been gored by an elephant, or bitten by a snake. He teaches us which trees are deadly."

"I didn't know there were any deadly trees in Chicago."

"There aren't. He says he's just preparing us in case any of us ever find ourselves in the Amazon."

"Where's the fun part?" my mom said.

"There *is* no fun part. It's not Kid*Fun*, it's Kid*Skills*. The only thing is I don't see is when I'm ever going to need any of these great skills I've got."

"I don't know. Sometimes I'm in my office, working on a patient and suddenly an elephant charges in. If you were there, you could carry me out on a litter."

This got me to smile at first, and then we both just cracked up.

"Why didn't you tell me it was this horrible?" my mom said through her laughter.

"I didn't want Wayne to think I couldn't handle it."

"Oh, don't mind Wayne. If he had any kids of his own, a lot of his big theories would get punctured in a minute. And whatever he thinks about it, we're pulling you out of KidSkills. It sounds more like Marine boot camp than an after-school program for kids. Are you sure, though, that you can afford to go through the rest of your life without the skills you would have learned in there?"

"It'll be hard, I admit. Next week we're supposed to learn how to treat jungle fevers with compresses made of leaves."

I really made my mom laugh with that one.

Later that afternoon, she called Ranger Jack and told him she was pulling me out of the program. Then I heard her calling Wayne. I was reading in the living room and didn't want to seem nosey, so I could only hear about half of what she was saying.

". . . but she hated it . . . Wayne, I don't really think Tory needs any toughening up . . . no, it's okay, it's not your fault."

A little while later, she came out and sat down next to me on the sofa.

"Wayne says he apologizes for giving you a bum steer."

"He did? He said that?" I had a hard time imagining Wayne apologizing to me. He seemed so stern, so ultra-adult.

"Yes. He admitted he has a lot to learn about parenting."

Parenting?! I felt the word flash through my head. I'd been right from the start — Wayne *was* trying to worm his way into our family and be my new dad. I felt my face getting red and then I just couldn't help it. I burst out, "I don't care if he does marry you. That still won't make him my father!"

"Whoa!" my mom said and took my hands. "Who said anything about anybody marrying anybody, or anybody being your new dad? Honey, I've only been out with Wayne a few times. He's a nice guy, and we like a lot of the same things. I don't feel about him anything like I did about your father, but I'm having fun. You can't begrudge me that."

"I guess not," I said in my sulky voice, a voice even *I* hate, even as I'm using it. But sometimes I just can't help it.

"So lighten up, okay?"

"Okay," I said, but I didn't feel like lightening up at all.

"And talk to me about what we're going to

do with you. I've pulled you out of KidSkills, but what are we going to do with you now?"

This changed my mood. I had my answer all ready. I'd had it for some time now.

"Let me be a latchkey kid! Lots of kids in my class are. The Burris twins. Cindy Tompkins. Lucy French, who I met at Peaceful Garden, called me this week and her mother's finally let her be one."

I expected her to say no, the way she did the other times I asked. But this time she said, "Let me think about it."

That was Friday. On Sunday afternoon, we were out shopping along Clark Street, and we stopped in a coffee shop that had little tables. My mom had coffee and I had cocoa and we both had big hunks of carrot cake. And then when we were done, she pulled this little velvet pouch out of her purse and put it on the table in front of me.

"Go ahead," she said. "Open it."

I didn't know what to expect, but whatever I couldn't have guessed.

"A key," I said. "The key to our house on a little silver ring. Which must mean . . ."

"Yes," my mom said, smiling a big smile. "You finally wore down my resistance."

"I'm a latchkey kid!" I said. "Yea!"

I guess I was a little loud because I noticed that several people around us in the coffee place were staring. I didn't really care. I was too happy. I walked home with my hand inside my pocket, curled around my key.

It was the first time in my life I felt kind of grown-up. I couldn't wait for Monday when my latchkeydom would officially start.

8

My mom is not usually a nervous person, but she was spinning like a top Monday morning when I got up for school and came downstairs for breakfast.

"Now here's a list of emergency numbers I've taped up for you," she said, pointing to the refrigerator door. I went over and took a look. There was the number of her office, which I already knew by heart. And 911. But there were about ten more. My grandma, who lives way up in Minnesota. The Poison Control Hotline.

"Mom! I'm eleven. I'm not going to be drinking the Drano."

"I know, I know," she said, putting a bowl in front of me and a box of cereal. "Now I'm sure you know not to let *anyone* in the house. If they say they're here to read the meter or anything like that, tell them to please come back another time." She stopped to mentally tick off a few things on her fingers, then added, "Oh, and if you smell smoke, or the smoke alarm goes off, you remember what to do from our fire drills."

I nodded.

"Let's see. I'm sure there's more, but I can't think of it now."

"Mom, I'll be all right."

"Will you call me as soon as you get here — so I know you got in?"

"Okay."

"And you've got your key?"

I held it up to show I had it, and then I gave her a hug and told her, "Mom, you won't regret giving this to me. I'm going to be the best latchkey kid there ever was!"

Well, I didn't quite make that goal.

I was so excited coming home. I let myself in with my key. That part was a breeze. I sat down on a chair at the kitchen table, but I was too excited about being a latchkey kid to just hang out. I felt like I should be doing something to show I was this new, super-mature, super-responsible person.

The wastebasket next to the sink was overflowing, and the cats' litter in the basement needed changing. I got both the garbage and the litter into one giant trash bag and put on my jacket and went out back to put the bag in the trash can.

I was trying to keep the cats in, and so pulled

the door shut behind me as I went out. I didn't even realize what I'd done until I'd come back and tried to get in, turning the doorknob left and right.

I was locked out!

I couldn't believe it. I reached for my latchkey, but I already knew it wasn't there. I peered through the window in the door and there it was, nice as pie, sitting in the middle of the kitchen table where I'd left it. So near and yet so far, as they say.

Then both cats — Calvin and Agnes — hopped up onto the counter and were twisting their little bodies so they could press their noses against the glass and look at me. If cats could talk, I knew they'd be saying, "What are you doing out there? Come on back in."

But I couldn't, of course. Instead I sat down on the back steps and put my head in my hands and tried to think.

It came to me right away. Mrs. Wade! She lives next door to us and my mom gave her an extra key a long time ago. For taking in packages and watering plants when we were gone. I practically flew over to her back door. I rang the bell and waited, and waited, then rang it again. I peered in through her window, but everything was dark inside. Then I remembered that she and Mr. Wade had gone to Florida on vacation and wouldn't be back for another week.

I snapped my fingers in disgust. Just my luck. I tried to think of some other way out of this gloomy situation, but there *was* none. None, that is, except for the one thing I wanted to do less than anything else in the world — go to my mother's office, tell her that within my first five minutes of being a latchkey kid, I'd managed to lock myself out of the house. But there was nothing else I could do.

When I got there, she was just coming out of her treatment room holding a square of X-ray film, and when she looked up and saw me, all my carefully prepared words came tumbling out as I told her what had happened.

"Oh, Tory, how could you?!" she said, clearly exasperated with me.

I was so embarrassed. I wished I could just disappear into a little puff of smoke instead of having to stand there with my mother looking at me as though I was a total idiot. Then she started shaking her head and said, "I don't know. Maybe you aren't ready for this much responsibility."

Suddenly I wasn't embarrassed anymore; I was insulted. I just couldn't believe that my mother had such a low opinion of me. I know — how could I be insulted at being thought dumb and irresponsible when I'd just done something so dumb and irresponsible? I don't know. But I just knew this was only one stupid mistake, that I could still do great as a latchkey kid.

"Please," I begged my mother. "Just give me one more chance. This was a fluke. You'll see. Please."

She sighed and looked totally exasperated, but she did give me her own key. "Try not to lose this one. Don't go outside once you're in there. Just wait for me to get home. Maybe I need to rethink this latchkey business. We'll talk later. Just don't do anything until I get there!"

But I couldn't not do *anything*. In fact, I knew I had to do just the opposite of that. I knew I had to do something spectacular to show my mother I was up to the challenge of latchkeying. I thought all the way home and came up with a fabulous idea. I'd fix a great dinner and have it all ready to surprise her when she got home. I looked at the grandfather clock in the hallway as I came in. I still had almost an hour until she got home. I hadn't really cooked much before, but I'd watched my mom a million times and, well, I just knew I could do it!

I took off my jacket and changed into my oldest jeans and a beat-up T-shirt so I could really get to work. In the kitchen, I opened the refrigerator and looked around inside. Plenty of lettuce and vegetables for salad. Up in the freezer there was a frozen quiche. I rubbed my hands together like a mad chef. This was going to work out great. Quiche and salad and what? Bread. But bread is so ordinary, I thought.

What about something more festive, more surprising?

I rooted around in the cupboards and came up with just the thing.

"Poptarts!" I told Calvin, who was standing on the counter, rubbing up against me. He clearly thought it was dinnertime for cats as well as people.

"In a minute," I told him. I had to get my meal started before I could think about kitty cuisine.

First I read the directions on the quiche box. It only had instructions for baking it in the oven. But my mom doesn't like me to use the stove when she's gone because it's gas and she's afraid I might start a fire. So I figured the microwave would have to do. It would probably work just fine. The company probably just hadn't thought to put those directions on the box. I put in the frozen block of quiche and set the timer for half as long as the oven time. Twenty minutes.

Then I set about making my salad. I pulled out everything I could find in the refrigerator that said "salad" to me. Lettuce. Carrots. Cucumbers. I cut them all up and put them in a big bowl. Nothing to it. I looked in. It looked okay, but not like a party salad, which was what I was trying for.

I went to the cabinets and found a little can of orange slices. Well, that would be unusual, and who ever said you couldn't put fruit in a salad? Then I found a jar of maraschino cherries in the door of the refrigerator and put a few of them in, too. They looked so colorful sitting next to the orange slices that I wound up just dumping in the whole jar. Now my salad was beginning to look like something. There wasn't any dressing, so I just mixed in about half a jar of mayonnaise. It looked a little gloppy, but still pretty good.

Then I put the Poptarts into the toaster slots and pushed down the lever. By now both cats were roaming the counter like little beasts just in from the jungle.

"Oh, you two!" I said, at my wit's end with them. "Okay. You win. I'll get you your food."

I put their empty food dish on the counter next to the salad. Then I rummaged around in the pantry and found a can of liver flavor cat food — their favorite — and went to dump it in their dish. But just then this most terrible smoke started pouring out of the toaster.

"My Poptarts are burning!" I shouted to the cats and dumping their food out of the can. I yanked the tarts out of the toaster and tossed them into the garbage. Luckily there were more in the package. I stuck two more in and made a mental note to keep an eye on them next time. The kitchen was pretty smoky. I threw open the windows so the smoke alarm wouldn't go off and the air would clear before my mother got home.

Then I went back to my salad and looked inside the bowl and screamed, "Oh, no!"

In my confusion over the burning Poptarts, I'd dumped the cat food right into the salad instead of into the cats' bowl. I heaved a big sigh and pushed the bowl out of the way, over toward the end of the counter. I'd deal with it later. Then I just about jumped through the ceiling when the explosion came.

"BOOM!"

I knew the sound all too well, having heard it on a few previous occasions. Microwave Implosion! I got up my nerve and turned around to see this gooey, eggy stuff creeping out the sides of the door of the microwave. My quiche!

Just then the back doorbell rang. I looked through the window and saw that it was Karen. My mom had said not to let anyone in, but I didn't think she meant to include Karen in that, and so I opened the door.

"Wow!" she said, looking around. "Did you call the President yet and have him declare this a National Disaster Area?"

"It's *that* bad, isn't it?" I asked and told her the stupid thing I'd done, locking myself out, and how I'd wanted to make dinner to prove I was up to the challenge of being a latchkey kid. I sat down at the table and put my head in my hands to weep. But Karen lifted me out of the chair by my arm.

"No time for tears," she said. "When's your mom due back?"

I looked up at the clock. "Any minute," I said despairingly.

"Well, let's just try to get the worst of this cleaned up. Maybe we can beat the clock. You — open the windows and wipe out the microwave. I'll put all these dishes in the dishwasher."

Just then I heard a terrible crash. Karen and I both spun around at the same time and saw Calvin hopping off the counter, where he'd given the salad/cat food bowl a good push, down onto the floor, where Agnes was already picking bits of cat food out from among the white mayonnaise sea dotted with lettuce and cucumbers and orange slices.

At this perfect moment, in through the door walked — my mom.

She took in the whole terrible, hideous, horrible mess with one long look. And then she looked at me. And then she looked at Karen and said to her, "I know you are Tory's best friend, and that you will probably grow up to be a wonderful adult. And even now I realize you may not be responsible for my kitchen looking like it's been under nuclear attack, but — "

Karen guessed what was coming next. " — but I'd better get out of here quick if I value my life. Gotcha, Doctor Scott. See you, Tore. And good luck!"

I was going to need more than luck. My mom didn't say anything for a long time after Karen was out the door. She stood there and kept looking around, like a tourist in front of some incredible sight.

"I wanted to make you dinner so you could see what a great latchkey kid I was going to be. Things just sort of got away from me, I guess."

"Oh, boy," she said, being as nice as she could. "I don't know, Tory. Maybe this latchkey idea's just not going to work out."

"Oh, Mom, it *will*! I just know it! I know it doesn't look good at the moment, but I know what I can do and I can be a great latchkey kid. Please just give me one more chance. Just give me tomorrow and if anything terrible happens, we'll call it off. You can get me a sitter. Send me back to Happy Hours even. Just one more chance is all I ask. One."

She sat down at the table and sighed.

"Oh, all right," she said.

(Yea!)

9

The next day Karen didn't come by (she wasn't dumb), and I didn't try to fix another party supper (I'm not dumb either), and so it was my first real day of being a latchkey kid — on my own.

When I came in I was full of trying to remember all my latchkey responsibilities.

"Got to call Mom at the office," I told the cats as I punched out her number on the kitchen phone. I actually liked doing this. It made me feel like we both had jobs to do and were sort of reporting in with each other. Plus I wanted to hear my mom's voice. There was something about coming into the house with her not there that had given me a gray sort of feeling. (At least the cats were there at the door to greet me so I didn't feel completely alone.) I figured that talking to Mom would take away some of my gloominess. All I got, though, was her voice on the answering machine. And then I remembered that Tuesday was her day being dentist over at the VA hospital.

As I put the receiver down, a flood of sadness swept over me. I felt like the loneliest kid in the whole world. I realized this was a little ridiculous, seeing as I'd been begging my mother for *weeks* to let me be a latchkey kid and here I was, caving in and feeling totally sorry for myself, now that I'd been one for all of one big day. Sometimes even *I* think I'm impossible.

I'll make a sandwich and then go watch some TV, I thought. I figured maybe I was just hungry and the place was too quiet. I made a peanut butter and jelly sandwich and wiped the counter so there wasn't a crumb in sight. I was going to do things absolutely right today. But then, as I was picking up the sandwich plate to head into the living room, I heard the weirdest thing. Or at least I could have sworn I heard it.

"Hey, Tory!"

It was Nell's voice.

"I'm here in the kitchen!" I shouted back, and both cats jumped a little. I realized that I was talking to no one. I was answering a phantom. Nell was in California. I was making her up because I missed her. She'd been my after-school pal. I had never been lonely when she was around, and now she was gone — happy with her daughter and her family while I was all alone. This made me so sad I didn't feel hungry anymore, and so I just put my sandwich in the refrigerator.

I didn't feel much like watching TV either. Or doing homework (this wasn't *as* weird since I never feel like doing homework). I just went into the living room and sat in the big wing chair waiting for my mom to get home.

This was restful for a little while — until I started hearing the footsteps. They were coming from the kitchen — soft and draggy, just the sort of footsteps a mummy in a horror movie would make, dragging his wrappers behind him, coming into the living room to put his curse on me. I knew I was imagining this, just as I'd imagined Nell's voice, but this didn't stop me from being frozen in the chair like an ice cube of fear.

I finally worked up enough nerve to tiptoe into the kitchen, and of course no one was there. The back door was locked, and the only sound was the tick-tocking of the old grandfather clock. And then the purring of Agnes, who'd jumped up on the kitchen counter next to me.

"Agnes," I said to her, "do you think I'm going nuts?"

I didn't say anything about any of this to my mom when she finally got home (about ten hours later, it seemed). I didn't want her to think I wasn't up to being on my own. It seemed kind of pitiful even to me that I was having trouble with such a simple little thing.

I stayed awake in bed that night after I'd supposedly gone to sleep. I was too wound up thinking all these negative sort of thoughts, getting madder and madder at myself. I mean, what was being a latchkey kid after all? Just hanging out for a few hours in the middle of the afternoon in your own house. This didn't seem like something that should be beyond me. Maybe I wasn't the mature eleven-year-old I thought I was. I always kidded Karen for being a big baby, but what was I being now? Maybe some kids are just braver, more sure of themselves than other kids, and I was in the wimp category. Tory the Wimp.

I managed to get through Wednesday and Thursday all alone, though, and although I was lonely and scared (the mummy came back a couple of times), I didn't let on. I was kind of trying to tough myself out, to see if I could make myself braver than I was. It was the only thing I could do, really. Either I'd somehow make myself into a latchkey kid, or I'd have to go back to another dinky after-school play group. Lonely and scared seemed better than bored and babied.

On Friday, when I was in the den studying, the back doorbell rang. I ran into the kitchen and saw that it was Karen, standing on the steps in her jean jacket. At first I was so happy to see her — someone to make the loneliness and scariness go away. But then I felt my heart sink. I remembered my mother had said not to let anybody in, and now I knew that anybody included Karen. Probably it especially *meant* Karen.

I opened the back door a little ways and said, "Hi."

"I didn't have anything special to do. I just thought I'd drop by," she said. For the first time this fall, it was cold enough to see your breath, and hers came out in light puffs as she spoke.

"Oh," I said.

"Aren't you going to let me in? I brought some new magazines. I thought we could talk about your hair." Karen thinks my hair — which I love — is way too old-fashioned. She always has some style in mind for me that involves shaving half of it and dying the other half purple.

"I can't," I said.

"You can't look at magazines?" she asked, not understanding.

"No, I can't let you in. My mom said I wasn't supposed to let anyone in while I'm being a latch-key kid."

"Oh," Karen said, pushing against the door (but I pushed back, gently). "She meant burglars and stuff. She didn't mean me."

"I think she might have specifically meant you," I said.

"But you don't know for sure."

"No," I had to admit. "But I don't want to take the chance of getting in trouble. This is my test week and I want to do this absolutely perfectly."

"What if I died of exposure standing out here in the cold? Would you take me in like a Good Samaritan, or would you gently push my fallen body outside and shut the door?"

"Oh, Karen, don't be silly."

"Who's being silly? It's cold out here. I could very well freeze to death while you're standing in your warm house treating me so badly. You'd regret this the rest of your life."

"I'd just have to live with it then, because I am not letting you in."

I thought we were just teasing back and forth, but then all of a sudden I could see that underneath, Karen was really hurt. I felt awful, but what could I do?

"I guess being a latchkey kid is more important to some people than having a best friend," she said and smiled, but it was a sad smile, if you know what I mean. She turned and began walking away.

"Karen?" I called, but then I couldn't think of anything to say, and so I just watched her walk away and around the house.

I went back into the den and flopped onto the sofa and got even more depressed than I had been. Maybe I'd been wrong all along. Maybe being a latchkey kid wasn't what I'd thought it would be. Here I was, lonely and scared and now on top of everything else, I was losing my best friend.

I didn't know where to turn. I didn't want to tell my mom. I couldn't talk to Karen about it. Then I had a thought. I got the phone book out of the desk drawer and found a number for Burris on Oakdale. The twins would probably be home, latchkeying themselves. Maybe they'd understand.

The phone rang twice and Michael answered. (I could tell it was Michael and not David because he said "hello" and not just "yeah.")

"It's Tory Scott," I told him. "I need your help. You and David. I'm not doing too terrifically at this latchkey business. Do you think we could meet after school on Monday? I could come to your house. I think I just need to talk to someone else who's doing it. Get some tips or something."

"You mean you need to *network*," he said. I'd heard my mom use that term when she called other dentists to ask their opinion on tricky cases.

"Yeah, networking — what a great idea!" I said. "Hey, I know. Would it be okay if I called Cindy Tompkins and asked her to come, too? And my friend Lucy French. She's another latchkey kid. Maybe we could all compare notes. I need all the help I can get."

"Okay," Michael said. "I'll ask my mom, but as long as Karen's not coming, I'm sure it'll be okay."

10

The next day at the lockers I told Karen about my stroke of genius.

"Networking," she said sarcastically. "How professional of you. Does this mean you're a professional latchkey kid? Is latchkeying your *career*?"

She was still mad — I could tell — about my not letting her in the day before. But what else could I have done? If I disobeyed my mom, she'd for sure take my latchkey away and I'd have to go to some new, dumb after-school group. It was as though Karen was asking me to risk this to be her friend. Which just wasn't fair.

I wanted to tell her this, but I couldn't. I knew she'd deny she was even upset. She's like that. She wants to seem so cool, even if she's really burning inside, or crying huge tears at night when nobody can see. (And she's as big a baby as me when it comes down to it.) But because she wants to seem so cool, I couldn't just put my arm around her shoulders and say, "Now, Karen. Don't be upset."

She'd just look blankly back at me and say, "Why, whatever do you mean?"

Being best friends with her is not the easiest thing in the world. I could see that I was going to have to keep a pretty low profile about anything that involved my being a latchkey kid. Since Karen wasn't one, she didn't want to hear that I *was*.

And so I didn't say anything more about getting together with the other latchkey kids after school that day. Besides, even if she wasn't teed-off at me, Karen would never get excited about any group. She thought all groups — except rock groups — were stupid. She was always making fun of the clubs they have at school.

"Oh, let's join Future Nerds (what she calls Future Scientists)!" she'd always say. "My heart is absolutely *pal*-pitating at the thought of it."

Actually, my heart *was* racing a little by the time I got to the Burris brothers' house. It was hard being a latchkey kid alone. Maybe if I could get together with other kids in the same boat, it would be less scary and lonely. This group might be the answer to my problems!

Everybody showed up. By four o'clock, there were five of us sitting around on the floor and furniture of the twins' living room. The twins and me and Cindy Tompkins and Lucy French. When

I'd called Cindy, she jumped at the idea of "networking" with other latchkey kids. She said she was dying for someone to gripe to about her experiences. This wasn't why I was organizing the meeting, but by then I'd already invited her, and I couldn't see any way of *un*-inviting her.

When I called Lucy French, her response was the exact opposite of Cindy's. She *loved* being a latchkey kid. For one thing, it had gotten her out of Peaceful Garden, which had been driving her nuts. But more important, she said, it gave her some private time every day. She told us more about this at the meeting.

"All day long I'm in school with a jillion kids. Then at night my parents are there. Saturdays I've got piano lessons. Sundays we go visit my grandma." She shook her mop head of brown curls and pushed her big glasses up on her nose. "My latchkey hours are the only time I have for *my* stuff — like writing in my journal, and practicing my piano lessons."

As she was saying this, I realized that time alone did have its good side. For instance, in the past week I'd done a lot more homework and wasn't as far behind in class, which made me feel better about life in general.

David Burris had gotten up and left the room while Lucy was talking. Now he came back with a six-pack of soda and a package of chips.

"My mom left these for our meeting," he said.

"She was happy Michael and I were getting together with some other latchkey kids."

"My mom was, too," I said. It turned out everybody's parents really liked the idea. Cindy was scowling at this, though.

"I know *my* mother wanted me to come hoping it would give me a better attitude about this whole latchkey thing," she said, pouting and tugging at the ends of her long, stringy blonde hair. "But I doubt that it will. I've been doing it for a year now, and I still don't like it, so what's going to change my mind? Maybe being with you guys will make it a little less awful, though." Cindy was twelve, but she was in sixth grade. She told us she'd had an operation on her back when she was seven, which held her back a year. "I guess that's when I kind of got used to my mother taking care of me at home." Cindy went on. "She made me gingerbread and did this great show with finger puppets."

"Yes," Lucy said, "but now you're older. Isn't it kind of neat, learning to take care of yourself?"

"I guess," Cindy said. Lucy was cheering me up a lot about being a latchkey kid, but Cindy wasn't going to be so easy to convince, I could see. Michael was somewhere in the middle.

"I think it's great being taken care of," he said. "Everybody likes that. But it's also fun testing yourself, seeing if you *can* do it on your own.

David and I try to make an adventure out of being latchkey kids. We've had our share of falling flat on our faces, though."

"Me, too," Cindy admitted.

Which got us all into telling our individual disaster stories. It was a relief to hear that everyone else had messed up, just like I had. Hearing them got me to confess the whole terrible saga of my Disaster Dinner, which got a laugh out of everyone. But then Michael said, "We could help you with that. We're expert microwave chefs by now."

"Well, *sort of* expert," David qualified his brother's bragging.

"And I'm a great shopper," Cindy said. It was the first positive thing she'd said so far. "I could show you all how to buy stuff at the supermarket, and the twins could show us how to put a meal together without totally destroying the kitchen."

"I don't know," I said. "My mom's birthday is next week, but I was just thinking of sticking a candle in a cupcake. I don't think I'm quite ready to make another dinner. Maybe when I'm thirty-five or so."

"Don't be silly," Lucy said. "You've got to get back on the horse that threw you."

"We can help," Cindy offered.

"It sounds like we need another meeting, then," Michael said. "A field trip to help Tory make her mother's birthday surprise."

"Does this mean we're a club?" I said. I was

half joking, but then everyone stopped talking and I could tell we were all thinking about the idea.

"Well, why not?" Michael said. "We could call ourselves The Latchkey Kids Society. We've already got our insignias." He pulled his key out of his pocket. We all did the same.

"Maybe we should call it The Latchkey Kids Society International," David said. "In case we feel like expanding later." Leave it to spacehead David to come up with the most totally impractical suggestion in the world. We all just looked at him thinking, Get real.

I thought about the group. Michael was the practical one, David the impractical. Cindy was my least favorite (too negative), and Lucy my most favorite. I liked how cheerful she was, and that she was twelve. I liked having two older kids in the group — her and Cindy. It made it seem more important. I didn't know if we had the makings of a great club, or anything, but at least everyone was behind the idea of being a group. (Especially me.) And we did have a real, important purpose for sticking together. Safety and strength in numbers, like they say. Maybe fun, too.

"All right then," Michael said. "I hereby proclaim us The Latchkey Kids Society — uh, International. Anything that happens to one of us happens to all of us."

"Right," Lucy said. "If any of us is ever in trouble, the others will come to his or her rescue."

"We need a secret handshake," David said.

"What about if we all just put our right hands together now in a giant handshake to seal our pact," Cindy suggested.

We all agreed and did just that, then laughed — I guess because we had to break away from being so serious.

Then Michael made our first plan.

"Let's say we meet on Thursday in front of the Treasure Island grocery store at three-thirty and start our first club project — Tory's Mom's Birthday Surprise!"

11

In gym the next day, Karen and I were on the same basketball team. Part of the time we were sitting on the bench being "reserves," and she started talking to me.

"I tried to call you yesterday afternoon, but the phone just rang and rang. What's the matter? Aren't you even allowed to get *calls* from a delinquent like me anymore?"

"I told you I was going over to the Burris twins'. For my networking. How can you forget something you made so much fun of me for?"

She didn't acknowledge this little dig. Instead, she just said coolly, "Oh, right. How'd it go?"

I couldn't help sounding enthusiastic. "Well, kind of great, actually. I think it's going to be a neat club."

"Club?! It's already a club?! You've gotten yourself into some dweebie club? Tory, I can't believe it."

I could tell that underneath everything, Karen was really feeling hurt and shut out. I knew I'd never get her to admit that, though. I decided to try anyway.

"Karen, I'm sorry you're feeling excluded, but — "

"Excluded!?" she said, as though I'd just said something *too* ridiculous. "Excluded from Future Locksmiths? Excluded from getting so much valuable experience using latchkeys?"

It wasn't a very funny joke, and since it was at my expense, I didn't feel I had to laugh. So I didn't.

Now Karen was hurt, and I was, too. And we couldn't talk about it. I didn't know how we were going to straighten out this mess between us. Just because I was a latchkey kid and she wasn't, just because I might have some new friends — none of it changed the fact that she was my best friend and always would be. But she'd act like I was being sappy if I said something like that. So instead we both had to sit in this awful deadly silence until Mrs. Hoban called me out on the court to play.

On Thursday, I was the second Latchkey Kid to arrive at the Treasure Island grocery store. Lucy was already there, sitting cross-legged on top of one of the newspaper boxes outside the front door. She was reading some sheet music for her piano lessons. She folded them up and stuffed them into her pink knapsack when she saw me.

"I envy you — being able to play the piano and all," I told her.

"It's a lot of work, but I want to become a concert pianist, and so I have to practice all the time. I like having this big dream of fame and fortune, though."

"I don't know *what* I want to be," I told her.

"That's okay. You're only eleven. You don't have to know yet."

"Being eleven's great," I told her. "Better than ten, way better than nine when my mom hardly let me do anything."

"Yeah. That's one of the things I like about being a latchkey kid, too. It's so grown-up. Cindy was complaining about not getting taken care of, but I really like it that I'm not just some big baby, that I'm helping out in my family. My mom and my dad both have jobs, and latchkeying is kind of *my* after-school job. Like, I've been putting in a load of laundry before I start my piano practice. That way, it's done and dried by the time my mom gets home from the library where she works. She really appreciates it. Then on weekends when she's off, I let her do stuff for me — like taking me for a haircut, or out to get clothes."

I nodded, then asked her a question I'd been too embarrassed to ask at the meeting, in front of everyone.

"But don't you ever get scared? Sometimes I . . . well, I hear noises."

"Like ghosts?"

"More like mummies."

"Oh. Well, I think you've just got to tell those mummies to get lost. They don't like to mess with latchkey kids, especially not members of The Latchkey Kids Society *International*. They know we're smart and tough, and *world-famous*."

I had to laugh along with her.

We were still laughing when I heard a familiar voice from just behind me.

"Tory, what're you doing here?" It was Karen, helping her mother with the grocery shopping. I said hi to them both. I knew she didn't mean what was I doing here, but what was I doing sitting here laughing and having a good time with this total stranger. She stopped for a minute while her mom went on into the store.

"Karen, this is Lucy French," I said, trying to be cool. "She's one of my latchkey friends."

"Nice to meet you," Karen said, with all the warmth you'd use in greeting a rattlesnake you met in the desert. "Well, I guess you two must have all sorts of important 'key' issues to discuss, if you know what I mean. Stuff I couldn't possibly relate to, so I'll just mosey along here with my mom."

And she was gone without so much as a good-bye. I could see the hurt on her face as she turned away. I felt awful, but there really wasn't anything I could do since I wasn't doing anything wrong. I just had to let her go. I felt tears hot and stinging in my eyes and tried to rub them away.

"Friend trouble?" Lucy asked me.

I nodded, but didn't say anything. She didn't either. Lucy's smart and I guess she understood how these things go and was nice enough not to make me explain.

"Ready, guys?" someone said, crashing into us at the same time. It was David. (He always called everybody "guys," even if they were girls.) He and Michael and Cindy were all together.

"You bet," I said.

"Well then," Michael said. "Let's get going. Let's see how you'd normally shop for your mom's birthday dinner. Get what you think you need and then we'll help you out if we think you can do better."

They got me a cart and sent me off on my own. I went up and down every aisle, trying to get stuff that looked good, *and* looked like I could make it. Once I ran into Karen and her mother in the frozen foods section and started to say something, but Karen just turned around and pretended to be studying the important differences between brands of peas. When I was done I wheeled up to the row of checkout lines where the rest of the Latchkey Kids were waiting. Michael and Cindy took over, peering into and poking through my cart. The Cart Inspectors.

"What's this?" Cindy asked, A giant-size bag of Cheezos, a carton of Extra-Calorie cherry-chocolate ice cream, eight microwave cheeseburgers, a big bottle of orange soda, and a pumpkin?!"

"Well, Halloween's next week and it was so cute and . . ."

"Makes sense," David said, nodding. I knew that if he thought this was a good idea, it probably wasn't.

"Tory," Michael said, in his most sensible voice. He was wearing a tie today and so looked like a junior store manager. "First off, does this look 'ike a menu that would appeal to a mother? I ⎯ it is *her* birthday."

⎯ d to admit I'd sort of picked stuff that *I* lik⎯ d.

"And is it nutritionally balanced?" Lucy asked.

"Probably not," I said sheepishly.

"It does have a lot of foods in the orange group," David said, pointing to the soda and the Cheezos and the pumpkin.

I laughed along with everyone else.

"Let's go through again," Cindy said. "All of us together this time. I'm a shopping expert. I've been doing it for my mom for a year now. I've even brought along coupons" — she pulled a fistful out of her backpack — "so you can save money on what you buy."

"And remember to always do your shopping in big stores like this. Don't go to the all-night mini-marts. They charge twice as much," Lucy added.

"And don't stand in the Ten Items or Less line when you've got a hundred items," Michael said.

It was fun going through the store with them. Michael pushed the cart while David hung onto the front. Lucy read all the ingredients on the packages we'd pick out. She and her parents were careful consumers, she said. Cindy was the budget-minded one in the crowd. She showed me how the store brand of something sometimes costs half of the big brand names. I think she was kind of enjoying showing off. She was becoming more of a Latchkey Kid than I thought she would.

When we were done, we had the supplies for a very nice meal — one I knew my mom would like. And one I could fix without either using the stove, or ruining the kitchen. We had two tomatoes and an avocado to make a salad. A box of microwave fried chicken. A package of dinner rolls.

I insisted on keeping my carton of Extra-Calorie chocolate-cherry ice cream, even though it wasn't sensible or on sale, just because it was my mom's and my favorite. Now all I had to do was make one thing at a time, follow the directions on the chicken box, not put cat food in anything, and I'd be fine.

The other Latchkey Kids walked me home and left me at the door with my sack of groceries. I waved good-bye to them and went inside and wove around Calvin and Agnes, who always tangle up my feet with their scurrying and purring when I come in.

I went into the kitchen and set out my ingredients on the counter. I did everything according to directions, went step by step and by five minutes to six, I had my dinner all ready. I set two places at the table and put the card I'd gotten earlier in the week on my mom's plate. Then I sat down at the table and waited. I expected to hear the door opening, followed by her footsteps, followed by her usual "Hi, Tory! I'm home!"

Instead I heard the sound of two voices, and then, seconds later, there was my mom, *very* not alone. Wayne was right behind her.

"Hi, honey," she said. "Since it's my birthday, Wayne's offered to take us out to dinner. Isn't that nice?"

Then she looked around and saw what I'd done. My chicken was on a plate, my salad was in a bowl on the table. I'd set out a little basket of rolls. Everything looked really nice. But there were only two places, and not really enough food for three people. My big surprise was going over like a lead balloon. Wayne kind of froze up (although he's so stony it's hard to tell when he's also freezing up). My mom started fluttering, which is what she does when she's in a situation that makes her nervous.

"Oh, Tory," she said. "What a wonderful surprise. You've done this all yourself! And for me!" I could tell she liked all the trouble I'd gone to, but at the same time what was she going to do about it with Wayne there?

"Tory, I didn't know I'd be interrupting anything by coming along," Wayne said. "Why don't I just leave you two to your celebration."

"Oh, Wayne," my mom said.

"Well, if you have a dessert that'll keep, maybe I could stop back in an hour and take you both out for some ice cream. We could even dress up and go someplace fancy."

I was really surprised that Wayne could be such a nice guy, coming up with a reasonable compromise. Plus I love going to fancy restaurants — something I've only done about twice in my life.

"It's okay by me," I said. My mom didn't say anything; she just kind of silently fluttered some more. Wayne left and my mom and I had my dinner, and she told me she thought everything I'd fixed was great.

Then we both went upstairs, giggling like maniacs while we got ready. I picked out my best outfit — a medium blue skirt and matching sweater with rose-colored flats to match the rose in the sweater. Mom decided on her black dress and red coat. When Wayne showed up again, he was wearing a cool charcoal gray suit with a pale blue shirt. I thought we all looked pretty good.

The restaurant Wayne picked was Ambria, which is one of the fanciest in town. It turned out he went to high school with the guy who's the headwaiter there and so got us a table even though we weren't having a whole dinner.

The dessert I picked was white chocolate mousse with raspberry sauce. It was incredible. I can't even describe it except to say that on the Dessert Spectrum of the Universe, it was at the absolute opposite end from the tapioca pudding they serve in our school lunchroom.

I was having a pretty good time. My mom was in a great mood. She'd really liked my dinner, and told Wayne all about it, and how competent and responsible I was getting in general.

"I think Tory's really going to make it as a latch-key kid."

I felt like I was in kind of a glow. That is, until the conversation got sticky. It started when Wayne, who could be cool for a while but not too long a while, asked me (as I knew he would) if I had a boyfriend.

"Not since Tom Prendergast asked me to marry him in the first grade," I said, trying to put an end to the dumb subject by joking around. But Wayne used this as an opportunity to get his own knuckleheaded two cents' worth in.

"I guess some guys just know right off the bat who they want to marry," was what he said. And as he said it, he took my mom's hand and gave her this Meaningful Look. And suddenly I felt like I was going to lose my white chocolate mousse.

"Uh, excuse me, please," I said as I dashed from the table, out into the hallway and into the ladies' room.

I stood in front of the mirror and soaked a towel in cold water and pressed it to my face and told myself, "This can't be happening."

I guess the ladies' room attendant — a middle-aged woman in a black-and-white maid's uniform — overheard me. We were the only two people in there. She came over and asked if I'd like to sit down on the little sofa they had in the lounge area, across from the makeup mirrors. And then she just sat down next to me and waited until I felt like talking.

"My mother's got a boyfriend," I finally told her through the tears I couldn't stop. "I think they're going to get married."

"Did they tell you that?"

"No. He just hinted that he wanted to marry my mom."

"Well, that's a few steps down the line, then. I wouldn't get too worried all at once. Do you like him?" she asked me.

"I don't know," I said.

She shook her head and said, "The thing about change is sometimes it comes whether we want it or not. Sometimes it's like a train barreling down the track toward you. Sometimes your only choice

99

is to stand in front of it and get run over, or hop aboard, even if you're not sure it's going in the direction you want."

I nodded and sniffled into the tissue she'd handed me.

"Well," she said, "you're going to have to go back out there sometime soon or they'll miss you. Put on a brave face."

"Okay," I said, but I didn't feel brave. I felt as far from brave as you can get.

12

I was writing a paper for history class on Amelia Earhart, the famous woman flyer. I had three books out of the library on her and I was trying to make a summary of her flying exploits. But I just couldn't concentrate. My mind was scattered in too many directions.

First, I was thinking about the letter I'd gotten that day from Nell.

Dear Tory,

How's the mushroom crop coming? Are we rich yet?

Seriously, I miss you so much you wouldn't believe it. I hope you've missed me, too, and haven't forgotten your old Nell now that you've got these new latch-key pals.

The club is a great idea, though. You really sounded happy in your last letter.

The good news is that Mary Beth's

*baby, Caitlin, is so beautiful and smart,
and already, by the length of her, looks
like she might be one of us (tall persons)!
Mary Beth wants me to stay on here for
a while. I can't say, what with winter
coming on, that I'm entirely sorry to be
in California. I was thinking, though,
that if I'm still here in June when you
get out of school for the summer maybe
you'd like to come visit me. I have my
own car and we could take a trip up and
down the coast. See a few sights. What
do you say? Think about it and ask your
mom.*

*And in the meantime, remember that
no matter how many miles there are between us, you're never more than an instant away from me in my thoughts.*

*XOXOXO,
Nell*

Nell was right. I *was* happier now that I'd met
the latchkey kids. And in spite of what Karen
thought, it was fun belonging to a club — to have
started a club, really. If I hadn't called the others
up that day, we wouldn't be a club now (if I do
say so myself).

We've decided to meet every week, discussing
a different latchkey problem or topic each time.
Loneliness. Scary things that could happen and

how to handle them. Advantages of being a latch-key kid. This topic business was Michael's idea, of course.

We also decided to rotate the meetings from house to house and all the parents went along with this. Well, Wayne didn't like it, but he's not my parent — not yet anyway! — and my mom told him she thought it would be fine. I talked with her the other night after we got back from the restaurant and were watching TV, just the two of us, snuggled up on the couch under our down comforter. I let her know how scared I was that she and Wayne might get married, and how I wasn't sure I liked him enough to have him for a stepfather.

"It hasn't gotten to that point yet. Not for me anyway. And of course I'll talk to you about it if it does. Even if it does come to that, Wayne could never change the way I feel about you," she said.

This was kind of comforting, but only kind of. It still left the whole Wayne issue up in the air, and this was another thing that was distracting me from Amelia Earhart. My mom said she'd let me know if things got more serious between her and Wayne, if they were closer to getting married. But she didn't ask my opinion on the matter. It's unfair that kids never have any say in these things. They should at least have *some* vote. Thirty-three and a third percent maybe. After all, they're going to have to live with these guys, too.

My vote on Wayne was NO. Not that I hated him or anything. Actually, there were moments lately when I actually kind of liked him in spite of his stiff, rocklike manner. But kind of liking him was a long way from wanting him as my new father.

Still another thing that was bothering me was Karen's jealousy about the Latchkey Kids. She was acting more and more like we weren't best friends anymore. She thought I liked the Latchkey Kids better, especially Lucy French, who's older and wears nail polish.(Karen and I aren't allowed yet.) It wasn't true, though. Karen would always be my best friend. It was hard making her see that, though.

The day before, she and I had gone to the Century Mall. Karen's dad gets his hair cut there and we shop around the stores while he's in the barber chair. The Century is one of our favorite places — a mall in what used to be an old movie theater. The shops are fun, and the shoppers are mostly teenagers, which is what Karen likes to pretend she is. But this time, Karen just wasn't into it. Even in the card shop, where we usually double over laughing at the funny ones, I hardly saw her crack a smile.

"Karen," I said finally, pulling her by the hand, forcing her to turn around and look at me, "please don't tell me nothing's wrong again when something clearly *is*."

But she still wouldn't say anything.

"If it's about the Latchkey Kids, let's talk about it. If you won't talk, how can we be friends?"

"Maybe we *aren't* friends anymore," she said, staring hard into my eyes as she said it.

Then, just at this awful moment, her father came into the store looking for us.

"Hey, you two," he said in this happy voice, "having fun?"

"Oh, yeah," Karen said, sarcastically. I didn't say anything. I couldn't with her father there. I didn't really know what to say anyway. The three of us rode back to my house in silence, her dad listening to a football game on the radio, the two of us looking out opposite sides of the car. I was getting so frustrated trying to keep Karen as a friend when she was always mad at me. Why couldn't she see that I could be friends with the Latchkey Kids, and still be *best* friends with her?

All these things were tumbling through my brain that afternoon, keeping me from making any real progress on my Amelia Earhart report. And then the last straw — Calvin and Agnes came up and started sitting on my papers and books, and purring.

"Oh, all right," I said to them, as though it was all their fault, even though it wasn't. "I'll quit and do some chores." I went down and tossed a load of my clothes into the washing machine, put in some soap, and turned it on. Then I took the dry towels out of the dryer and folded them. Then I went back upstairs to take out the garbage.

I put on my down jacket. It had gotten cold early this year. It had rained the day before and the rain had frozen on the ground. I was going to put on my big tread boots, but then it seemed like an awful lot of trouble to go to, just to run the garbage through the backyard, out to the trash can in the alley. I'd just zip out in my tennis shoes.

This turned out to be my *big* mistake.

Maybe it was that the bag was so bulky and heavy, but when I hit the first slick, icy patch I lost my balance and went flying over the ice, onto a patch of concrete walk and smack into the high wooden fence that surrounds our yard.

All of a sudden I was flat on my back in pain. I felt something warm trickling down my forehead. I reached up and touched it. When I brought my fingers in front of my eyes, I felt a shock. It was blood. *My* blood.

But that's not where the big pain was coming from. It was my arm. I tried to lift it to touch my forehead and a giant bolt of pain seared from my fingertips up to my shoulder. I let the arm rest on the ground and looked. It was lying at a funny angle — I mean the funny thing was that it *had* an angle. Where it was normally two bones, it was now three — with one elbow and another angle midway between my elbow and my wrist. Just looking at it, I suddenly felt like I was going to throw up.

I screamed for help. Then I waited. Dead silence. I screamed again. Nothing. Nobody.

I looked up toward the house. I could see both cats sitting on the kitchen windowsill looking at me with wide eyes. It seemed like such a long way between me and the back door, especially if my only way of getting there was crawling. But what else could I do? If I waited there, I might freeze.

I tried to stand. It hurt so much I couldn't believe it. Even just moving my foot made it much worse. I looked down and saw that my ankle was big as a baseball. I thought I might feel sick again.

I fell back onto the sidewalk and figured out that I probably had a nasty cut on my head, a broken arm, and a sprained ankle. At that point I just wanted to lie there and give up. But I knew our neighbors were all at work. Help might not come for hours. I had to get into the house if I was going to get to the phone and call for someone to rescue me.

I began to move, pulling myself forward with my good arm, trying to stay off my bad ankle. With all these problems, I could only crawl a few inches at a time. I don't know how long it took me. I had to stop several times along the way until I could bear moving again. My elbow was getting scraped on the cement, but that was a small worry compared to everything else. One good thing was that the blood coming from my head seemed to have dried up.

I just kept looking at the cats for comfort. At least two furry creatures were there on the other side of the window, rooting for me to make it. If only I could.

Finally I got back to the steps. The hardest part was still ahead of me — somehow I had to drag myself up five cement steps. This took almost as long as crossing the whole backyard. Then when I'd gotten to the top, I still had to lean against the railing and pull open the storm door and pull myself up enough to reach the lock — all with one arm.

I struggled to pull my key out of my pocket and managed to get it into the lock. I pushed the door open and crawled across the kitchen floor to the phone. Unfortunately, our kitchen phone is on the counter. Usually this is no problem, but at the moment, from where I was, it looked a hundred feet above me. I knew I'd never be able to hoist myself up to reach it. Lucky for me, though, it was on the edge — half on/half off the counter.

"Calvin!" I shouted. "Agnes. Come here, sweeties." They were always pushing things off the counter for fun. I thought maybe I could get them to do it on purpose this time. But although Agnes came over and licked my bloody face and Calvin (the knucklehead!) actually climbed up and sat on my shoulder and started purring, they clearly had no idea what I really *needed* them to do.

I looked around for something to throw. I

opened one of the bottom cabinets and found a can of beans. Rolling onto my side, I grabbed it out of the cabinet with my good arm, rolled back away from the counter, and tossed the can. It worked! Down came the can and after it, the phone, both clattering onto the floor a few feet away from me.

I grabbed for the receiver and punched out the number of my mom's office. It rang, then rang again, then there was a click.

"You have reached the office of Doctor Barbara Scott, the Friendly Dentist. I am out of the office at the moment. Please leave your name and number after the beep, and I'll return your call as soon as possible."

Rats. I suddenly remembered that she was going to be at a conference that afternoon. She wasn't supposed to be home until seven o'clock or so.

I set the receiver down and started to cry huge, silent tears. All the way across the yard, all I'd thought of was getting to the phone so I could reach my mom and get her to save me. It hadn't occurred to me that she might not be there. Now I couldn't think what to do. In my panic, all my latchkey know-how just deserted me. I'd never felt so alone or helpless in my life. All I could do was roll onto my back and let out this terrible wail. And then, just at the exact moment I stopped, the phone next to me began ringing.

13

I picked up the receiver.

"Tory?"

"Lucy?" I gasped.

"What's wrong? Is that you? Did I call at a bad time?"

"No!" I shouted. "Don't hang up!"

"I'm not going to. Why would I? What's wrong? Just calm down and try to tell me."

But I couldn't be calm. The whole story came tumbling out in a rush. I couldn't get control of my words to make them make sense. "Garbage . . . slipped . . . ice . . . hurt . . ." was all I could manage between the huge sobs that were coming out of me now that I'd finally reached someone who could possibly help me.

"Tory. I'll call the others. We'll be right there. Just hang on!"

I held onto the receiver even after she'd hung up. It was the only connection to the outside world I had, and I guess I didn't want to let it go. I put my mouth up close to it and — even though no one was on the other end — whispered, "Please get here fast."

I didn't have to wait long — ten minutes maybe — until I heard someone trying to get in the front door, then running off and around the house. Then the footsteps were at the back door, then rushing across the kitchen floor. I looked up and heaved a sigh of relief.

"Lucy!" I looked at her and felt safe and happy — for one second. Until she let out the biggest shriek and then screamed, "Oh, Tory! You look awful!"

I must've looked upset, because then she pulled herself together a little and dropped to the floor next to me.

"Oh, boy. What a rotten paramedic I'd make. Here I am, trying to be cool in an emergency and I'm screaming like a banshee. Can you forgive me? It's just that I've never seen an accident victim before. I just know you're going to be fine, though."

I wished I didn't know that Lucy was the world's biggest optimist. I didn't know whether or not to believe her. My guess was that I probably looked terrible and she didn't think I'd be fine at all. She probably thought I was going to croak in about three seconds. I felt much worse looking at myself through her wide, horrified eyes.

"The others will be here in a few minutes. Michael took first aid at his summer camp, so he'll know what to do. Meanwhile, why don't I just try to clean you up a little?"

She didn't wait for me to answer, just went into the little bathroom off the kitchen. I could hear her fishing around in the medicine chest, and then she was back.

"I brought some iodine to clean up that cut on your head," she said, and began dabbing at it.

"Ouch!" I said.

"Oh, well, this is good news," she said, ignoring my protests. "Now that I've got the blood off, this cut's not nearly so gruesome, not really that big at all." She started putting Band-Aids on it. When she'd put on about five, I said, "I thought you said it wasn't that big."

"Well, it's not a paper cut, either. But if this is the worst of it . . ."

"It isn't," I tried to tell her. "The worst is my arm and my ankle."

"What about your ar — ?" She didn't even get the whole word out. By that time she'd already looked and seen what I'd seen when I first saw it — an arm in three distinct parts instead of two. I guess it must have been too much for her. Anyway, the next thing I knew, my brave rescuer had gone into a swoon and fainted before my very eyes. (Good thing she hadn't seen my ankle.)

"Hey! Who's the injured one here?" It was Michael. He and David had just rushed in through the door and I suppose they must have been confused by two of us lying there side by side in two separate heaps.

"Lucy just looked at my arm," I said. "I guess it was too much for her."

"I'll take care of her," said Cindy, who was close behind the Burris twins. "Where does your mother keep her cleaning supplies?"

I waved in the direction of the cabinet under the sink. She found the bottle she was looking for.

"Ammonia," she said. "It usually works in situations like this." I didn't have the energy to ask how she had any experience with situations like this.

She poured a little onto a dish towel and held the towel under Lucy's nose and almost immediately Lucy was going "Wha . . . ? Huh?" Just like people who faint in movies.

Meanwhile Michael and David — who weren't squeamish at all — were looking over my arm.

"It's definitely broken," Michael said, "but I guess you already knew that. The ankle is only sprained, I think. David," he said to his brother, "can you get as much ice as there is in the freezer? I'll go get a couple of bath towels." He turned around. "Cindy, can you run outside and hail a taxi? Just hold it in front of the house."

"Okay," she said, propping Lucy against the kitchen cabinets. She was coming out of her fog by then and looking around.

"Oh, Tory," she said when she saw me. "I'm just a wimp."

I had to laugh, in spite of my pain. "It's lucky you've got that musical talent," I told her. "You'd never be able to have a career in medicine."

"What's your doctor's name, Tory?" Michael asked me as he and David tied ice-filled towels around both my arm and ankle.

"Doctor Kelson. The number's up there on the refrigerator."

"Lucy, call and tell him what's happened," Michael said.

I heard Lucy talking to someone on the other end and then she hung up and told us, "His nurse says he's at Saint Joseph's Hospital this afternoon. She'll call him and tell him we're on our way over. Hey, Saint Joseph's — that's only a few minutes away!"

"Great," Michael said, then turned to the others. "Now let's get Tory out to the cab."

Very carefully, the three of them hoisted me up onto my good foot. Michael had my good arm draped over his shoulder. Lucy was standing on my other side with her arm around my waist. David held the back door open for us, left a note for my mother telling her where we'd gone, then took my latchkey and locked up behind us.

With two friends supporting me, it was a lot easier to move. We got out front and Cindy had a taxi waiting. It was a little hard getting in with my bad ankle, but they made it as easy as possible, hoisting me through the door, easing me onto the seat.

"Where you kids going?" asked the driver when we were all inside. Michael and Cindy and Lucy arranged themselves around me in the big backseat, while David got in up front with the driver.

"Saint Joseph's Hospital," Michael said. "Emergency entrance." They were all acting so adult and capable that even though I was still scared about the pain, I felt safe and knew the Latchkey Kids would get me to the doctor as fast as anyone in the world could.

The drive went by in a blur. The next thing I remember we were in front of the emergency entrance and paramedics were coming out with a wheelchair to take me inside. I waved a little goodbye to the Latchkey Kids as the receptionist told them they'd have to stay in the waiting room.

Then I was on a table in an examination room and a nurse came in, followed by Dr. Kelson. He's been my pediatrician since I was born, so I felt relieved to see his familiar face. He asked what happened and I told him.

"My. I'm impressed that you were able to get back into the house, given the extent of your injuries. You're a brave girl, Tory."

I blushed and mumbled, "Thanks."

"Well, let's see what the damage is," he said, then asked, "Who put these ice packs on?" I clenched up. What if this was the wrong thing to do? I didn't want to get the Latchkey Kids in trouble, so I just said, "Oh, just some friends."

"Well, they did a very capable job," he said as he unwound them. "Probably saved you a lot of pain. People who know what they're doing are a big help to the medical professional." Then he stopped for a second. "But why didn't your mother do this? And why isn't she here now?"

"I tried to call her, but all I got was her tape. She's at a conference."

"Mrs. Higgins," he said to the nurse. "Will you have someone at Reception keep calling Doctor Barbara Scott until she can be reached? Tell her that Tory's here, safe and sound, and only broken in one place."

"Is it really broken?" I asked.

"Mmm-hmm," he said, inspecting my arm carefully. "And I want to get an X ray before I set it, but my guess is it's an angulated fracture and won't take all that long to mend. You can look at it as a badge of childhood. Almost everyone breaks a bone sometime or another. Now you'll have a story to tell for the rest of your life." I hadn't thought of it that way.

The X ray was easy. The setting of the bone — which really means snapping it back into place —

hurt a lot, but only for a split second, and then it was over. And then Dr. Kelson and the nurse were wrapping my arm up in cotton, then wet strips soaked in plaster, which would harden into my cast. My ankle got a soft cast, which would come off in a few days. My forehead got two stitches and my scraped elbow got a giant Band-Aid.

By the time I came back out into the waiting room, I was walking with a cane, but on my own! I felt all patched together again. Plus Dr. Kelson had given me a pill for the pain, and so I was feeling a lot better.

The Latchkey Kids stood up and gave me a little cheer as I came out. Karen was with them.

"But how did you . . . ?"

"I called her," Lucy said. "You told me she was your best friend and so I thought for sure she'd want to be here."

I could see Karen smile at this, and she gave me a big hug, which she's usually too cool to do.

I looked up and saw my mother and Wayne rushing through the double doors of the emergency entrance. She looked around wildly, and as soon as she spotted me, she burst into tears and rushed over.

"My baby!" she wailed. "I can't stand seeing you like this."

If she thought I looked bad now, she should have seen me a couple of hours earlier, bloody and crawling across the backyard. By comparison, I thought I was probably looking pretty good now. I didn't want to upset her even more by telling her this, though. I just let her hug me and cry some more as I tottered there on my cane. I couldn't hug her back too well on account of only having one hug-capable arm, but I did the best I could.

"I should never have left you alone," she said between sobs.

"Why do you say that? I could've slipped even with you there, and I couldn't have gotten better emergency care than the Latchkey Kids gave me."

"She's right," said Dr. Kelson. "Those friends of hers did a first-rate job of diagnosing her condition, keeping her swelling down, and getting her over here as fast and as safely as possible. If we gave prizes for this sort of thing, they'd get a blue ribbon."

I could tell my mom was impressed. She listened and nodded and took a tissue out of her purse to blow her nose. When she'd stopped crying and calmed down, she said, "It looks like you're really growing up, Tory. You and your friends handled a tough situation smoothly. I'm proud of all of you." Turning to the Latchkey Kids she said, "I want to thank you all for what you did for Tory. I'm really impressed."

"Yes," Wayne said. "Where did you all learn to

be so responsible and efficient? You must've gone to KidSkills."

"Oh, Wayne," I said, exasperated and blushed as I looked at the ground, embarrassed for him. But then I looked up and saw he was joking — a rare thing for Wayne, as far as I knew. It was kind of weird. Then he went on in his more usual voice, "But seriously, Tory, I want to be the first to admit I had doubts about you being a latchkey kid, but now I take back every one of them. You and your friends are clearly ready for the challenge of pre-teen responsibility."

Whew, I thought. Somehow it was a relief that he was back to his old, stuffy self. At least this was the Wayne I was used to.

Then my mom dragged him along with her, off to the desk to talk to my doctor. I was getting tired, and so let Karen help me down into one of the waiting room chairs. The Latchkey Kids were off talking with the paramedics, who were showing them some stuff about getting patients onto stretchers and tying on tourniquets. So Karen and I had a little space to ourselves.

"Boy, are you a mess," she teased me.

"Thanks," I said sarcastically.

"I hear the Latchkey Kids were practically as good as doctors."

"I was lucky they were there for me."

"I was surprised when Lucy French called me

and said you'd want me to know, seeing as we're best friends." She stopped and bit her lower lip. It looked like she was trying to keep herself from crying. "Is that still true?" she asked me.

"Of course," I said.

"But I've been so snobby about the Latchkey Kids. And I wasn't even around to help in your crisis."

"You would've if you'd known. You would've been the first to rush over."

"But then you wouldn't have been allowed to let me in," she teased.

I hit her on the arm for being such a brat and we both laughed. It was one of those moments when you just feel relieved, when you know you've gotten through some bad patch, and are on the other side now.

"I guess as clubs go, they're not all that bad," she said.

I couldn't believe my ears. Was it possible she wanted to join?

"You know, maybe you'd like to hang out with us in an unofficial way. I mean technically you can't be a Latchkey Kid, but maybe you could be our consultant, the way your dad's a consultant to those companies he works with."

I don't know what I expected. Did I really think ultra-cool Karen would get all excited or kiss my hand in gratitude? Not really. And so I wasn't all that surprised when she said, ultra-coolly, "I'll think about it."

We didn't have any more time just then to talk about it because my mom and Wayne were back, and then the Latchkey Kids. My mom had an idea.

"How about a treat for the best club I know? Dinner at Pablo's Mexican restaurant!"

Everybody cheered as we left the emergency room. And the whole way over to the restaurant, my new friends scrambled over each other (and me!) to autograph my cast with a felt-tip pen. After their names, they each added the initials L.K.

Latchkey Kid.

After dinner, Wayne dropped me and my mom off at our house. She ran me a nice hot bath, and helped me get into it, which was no easy trick. I had to keep my arm cast up on one side of the tub, wrapped in plastic wrap. Plus I had to hang my leg out over the other side so my ankle cast would stay dry.

When I was done, my mom got out my warmest flannel pajamas and propped me up in bed on scads of pillows. Then she sat all curled up at the foot of the bed in her quilted robe and down slippers. Calvin and Agnes (who can't stand to be left out of anything) hopped up, too, so it was a pretty crowded bed. I didn't mind. I was warm and sleepy, and feeling safe and sound.

"Snug as a bug in a rug," I said to my mom. It was something she used to say to me when I was little and she was tucking me in at night.

"Boy, this sure has been some day for you," she said, and I had to agree. One of the scariest, weirdest days, but in the end, everything had turned out all right. I was proud of the Latchkey Kids, and, I must admit, kind of excited at having been rescued so dramatically. Plus Karen and I were best friends again. Plus Wayne . . . what about Wayne, though?

"What about Wayne?" I said out loud to my mother.

"What about him?"

"Are you going to marry him?"

"I don't know."

"He wants to marry you."

"I know, but that doesn't mean it's going to happen. We haven't known each other all that long. Some things about him I really like. Other things, I don't."

"Like how stuffy he is," I inserted helpfully.

"Yes, like that. There are moments I'd like to strangle him with his necktie. But other times I really enjoy his company. I think this is one of those situations where time will tell, as they say. But nothing's going to happen overnight."

"But if you *do* marry him," I said, "everything's going to change around here."

"Everything's changing around here anyway," she said. "I was just thinking on the way home how sometimes you still seem like my little girl, but more and more lately, you seem like you're on your way to becoming a young woman. Pretty soon you'll be in high school, then college, then who knows where? I think we're both going to have to be open to a future filled with changes."

"Think we can handle them?" I asked.

"If we keep talking with each other, keep being friends as well as mother and daughter, I think we can." Then she said, "Hey," and hopped off the bed, over to my desk where she grabbed a marker. "I didn't get to autograph your cast before. Mind?"

"Go ahead," I said pulling my arm out from under the covers. I watched as my mom found a white space and drew a picture of a key and signed her name underneath. Then, under that she wrote *Very Proud Latchkey Mom.*

APPLE*PAPERBACKS

Pick an Apple and Polish Off Some Great Reading!

NEW APPLE TITLES

☐	MT43356-3	**Family Picture** Dean Hughes	$2.75
☐	MT41682-0	**Dear Dad, Love Laurie** Susan Beth Pfeffer	$2.75
☐	MT41529-8	**My Sister, the Creep**	
		Candice F. Ransom	$2.75

BESTSELLING APPLE TITLES

☐	MT42709-1	**Christina's Ghost** Betty Ren Wright	$2.75
☐	MT43461-6	**The Dollhouse Murders** Betty Ren Wright	$2.75
☐	MT42319-3	**The Friendship Pact** Susan Beth Pfeffer	$2.75
☐	MT43444-6	**Ghosts Beneath Our Feet** Betty Ren Wright	$2.75
☐	MT40605-1	**Help! I'm a Prisoner in the Library** Eth Clifford	$2.50
☐	MT42193-X	**Leah's Song** Eth Clifford	$2.50
☐	MT43618-X	**Me and Katie (The Pest)** Ann M. Martin	$2.75
☐	MT42883-7	**Sixth Grade Can Really Kill You** Barthe DeClements	$2.75
☐	MT40409-1	**Sixth Grade Secrets** Louis Sachar	$2.75
☐	MT42882-9	**Sixth Grade Sleepover** Eve Bunting	$2.75
☐	MT41732-0	**Too Many Murphys**	
		Colleen O'Shaughnessy McKenna	$2.75
☐	MT41118-7	**Tough-Luck Karen** Johanna Hurwitz	$2.50
☐	MT42326-6	**Veronica the Show-off** Nancy K. Robinson	$2.75

Available wherever you buy books...or use the coupon below.

- -

Scholastic Inc., P.O. Box 7502, 2932 East McCarty Street, Jefferson City, MO 65102

Please send me the books I have checked above. I am enclosing $_____ (please add $2.00 to cover shipping and handling). Send check or money order — no cash or C.O.D. s please.

Name_____

Address_____

City _____ State/Zip _____

Please allow four to six weeks for delivery. Offer good in the U.S.A. only.
Sorry, mail orders are not available to residents of Canada. Prices subject to change.

APP1089